A Funny Thing Happened On My Way to Hereafter

by
Michael N. Raskin

Cork Hill Press
Carmel

CORK HILL PRESS™

Cork Hill Press
597 Industrial Drive, Suite 110
Carmel, IN 46032-4207
1-866-688-BOOK
www.corkhillpress.com

Trade Paperback Edition: 1-59408-394-0

Library of Congress Card Catalog Number: 2006921715

1 3 5 7 9 10 8 6 4 2

Chapter One

I met a traveler from an antique land
Who said: Two vast and trunkless legs of stone
Stand in the desert. Near them, on the sand,
Half sunk, a shattered visage lies, whose frown,
And wrinkled lip, and sneer of cold command,
Tell that its sculptor well those passions read
Which yet survive, stamped on these lifeless things,
The hand that mocked them and the heart that fed:
"My name is Ozymandias, king of kings:
Look on my works, ye Mighty, and despair!"
Nothing beside remains. Round the decay
Of that colossal wreck, boundless and bare
The lone and level sands stretch far away.

(Ozymandias, by Percy Bysshe Shelley)

What the hell ever brought that to mind? I'm just sitting
here, staring at my computer screen, and, suddenly, I can *see*
the poem, <u>Ozymandias</u>, playing out in front of me.

Gee! I haven't read *that* one since I was in grade school...maybe fifth grade. But, I *do* remember that, each time I did read it, I would always find myself standing in the middle of some vast, empty space, and looking about me for any signs of life...any sign at all. That's the theme of that recurrent dream I used to have, around the age of five or so...Do you hear *that*, Freud? Just another crack in the foundation on which I've built my castle.

There are all those images of me being house-bound, all those little medical problems that tied me to the house, and to the emptiness "that" involved. I was left immobilized and isolated, and yearning to join the parade that passed before my window each day.

It's as if Percy Shelley had me in mind with that poem. But, what brought it back to me, now, when I'm in my fifties, and just sitting here, in my office? What is it that I always ask my patients to do in this kind of circumstance?

Oh, yeh! "What was your internal dialogue just before this hit you?"

Let's see, I was playing a game of solitaire on the computer, just wasting some time while I waited for my next victim...I mean, patient...to show for their appointment. I was listening to the news on the radio. The radio news; well, *that's* always depressing...Maybe *that* caused my mind to grow legs, traveling from idea to idea on its own. My job seems to be just following blindly behind, and attempting to put words to those images, as they appear.

I was *bored*, and I followed the path of least resistance. It really involves very little strain. The whole thing operates independently of any conscious control.

So, what could have been floating around in that great vacancy of a mind, as I was reciting the vacant threats cast by an errant grain of sand, in some far-off desert? Could I be so grandiose as to see myself as Ozymandias? Or, maybe, it was that grain of sand? There really is no difference, if you step back, and take a look. Despite all of his shouting and chest-beating, Ozzy doesn't appear to be any more powerful, or significant, than one of those grains of sand!

But, wait a minute! What could bring me to those empty boasts...those vacant threats...all that useless bravado?

That's it! I remember now! I was listening to some political advertisement on the radio, just following the news.

What part of it sent me on that specious tour of my mind?

Six of one...a half dozen the other.

Let's see, I was glancing at the headlines in the paper at breakfast, at the restaurant; what may it have been that was echoed on the radio? None of it ever adds up to any more than just blowing in the wind, anyway...I hope Dylan doesn't mind that allusion to his song.

What news? Is there *ever* any *good* news? I can remember my father, picking up what he used to call the "daily rag," and saying, "Let's take a look and see who's been raped, robbed, or shot today". That memory must go back to the Korean War era...or, did they define that one as a "police action"...you know, the way they tried to pawn off the "Vietnam Conflict"!

That was followed by an era of the Cold War, something of a battle of ideologies, this one being between those "Commie Pinkos" over in Russia, and us, you know, the "Good Guys," in the "Free" world. *Those* were the good old days; you knew who your enemy was, back then. Many a speech was made to denounce the unacceptable suppression of thought and belief, and the oppression of independence, which was occurring *over there*, in Asia, and then spreading around the world.

And, who could ever forget those great rebels, like Fidel Castro? Didn't America, and the rest of the Free World, support him and his "Freedom Fighters"? Man, *that* was drama; I mean, the way they fought for their liberation, against those tyrants and fascists, like Batista. It was reminiscent of Zapata, in Mexico...Viva Zapata!...only, Castro really won!

Hey, wasn't that really a shocker for *us*, I mean, the way he just whipped around, and gave us all "the finger," declaring himself a commie! Boy! I guess that taught *us* a lesson, huh? Since then, we've hardly ever done anything stupid like *that* again; you know, getting involved with some local civil disturbance, that really wasn't any of *our* concern in the first place. Unless, of course, you consider the events in Central America, or Southeast Asia, or Northern Ireland, or Yugoslavia, or Romania, Iran, Iraq, Lebanon, Afghanistan, Pakistan, Africa...Oh, you know!

So, what is it that seems to get our bowels into such an uproar?

Let's see. In Ireland, the Catholics are attempting to introduce the Protestants to *their* God, by their own version of "special delivery". In Central Europe, the Moslems and Christians are fighting to see which will dominate the other, a process which has been labeled "cultural cleansing". I guess, in a case like that, God may be perceived as Mr. Clean! In the Middle East, we have the Islamic jihad, which has defined its task as the conquest of the rest of the world.

For each, the message is always the same: God is great...God is love...and, if you dare to disagree with me, I will send you to meet his power, on a *personal* level.

Each of us...humans, that is...seems to seek his own way of expanding his little grain of sand, in a manner which will guarantee that each will, somehow, be remembered. I remember a book by Geoffrey Parrinder, <u>World Religions</u>, published in 1971, which made the statement that "**The problem of death is the beginning of philosophy**". I guess that's very profound. Think about it. It's our way of shouting out in the dark, and letting others know that we're here. It's a way of scratching your name into the very surface of this Earth, so it won't be erased. It is a way of seeking some sense of value to life, of giving some purpose to all the effort it takes just to *survive* in this world. It's our way of carving our name into the Tree of Life; of shouting, "Hey! Look over here! Here's proof that I was *here*!"

All of this, taken together, can be wrapped up in the cloak of "religion". I guess one could say that *religion* is that area of philosophy, which has evolved into a "system of beliefs," usually involving some kind of code of "ethics," and some established and defined standard of moral conduct. It is meant to be a system by which one learns to survive in this world, and to get the most out of it along the way; hopefully, without stepping on too many toes.

Most such systems are based on the concept that all men are basically equal. If that is true, of course, then religion should have, at its core, a means by which *all* men could "share" that experience of life.

Religion, in and of itself, doesn't seem to have been too bad an idea; but, where did all the killing come from? Nary a group has declared its thoughts, as a separate entity from the mass which is Man, that someone hasn't tried to stop it.

Words don't kill.

Ideas don't kill.

People kill!

The formula then becomes clearer. All one has to do is to take an idealistic philosophy, and just add that new magic ingredient...*civilization*...and the results will be **WAR**!

Where did all of this start to go wrong? What ideas could there have been which serve as such a lure to the human will; and how did they become so distorted?

These were the thoughts which captivated my mind, as I leaned back in my seat, and rested my head...for just a moment...on the back of that nice, soft comfortable, leather chair.

The room gradually became more and more quiet, except for the sound of that heating vent, and there was the flickering of the computer screen in front of me. I took a deep breath, and I opened my mouth, letting the air out very slowly; and I could feel my stomach slowly sink, as I fell even deeper into the chair.

Gradually, the glare from the radio began to sound further, and further, away. From the view outside the large front window, I could see that the Sun was just beginning to set. I could hear the last of the commuter traffic driving up Main Street, on their way home for the evening.

And everything was moving slower...and slower.

Chapter Two

Z-Z-Z-Z-z-z-z-z-z-z-z-z-z-z-z-z-z-z-.....

Huh! Uh! What...Where am I?...What time is it?

Geez, I must have dozed off!

So, I decided to take a look around me; and you know what? When I turned toward the bookcase...the one just under the window of the office...it wasn't there. So, I figured I'd check out the time; but the *clock* wasn't there. What am I saying, the clock; the *window* wasn't there! Or the wall in which the window was placed!

Something in my head told me, 'Toto, we're Not in Kansas, anymore"; and I tried to clear the cobwebs from my eyes.

What else was missing? Well, for one thing, I didn't note that refined stale smell of old and musty books, or the dusty carpet. I didn't notice that dingy darkness of the high ceilings and the rough-painted walls, a dirty shade of what was once white. It was still that wonderful dimness of an old building; but, somehow, there felt as if there was a greater expansiveness to it now.

So, I rubbed my eyes again, and tried to refocus.

Where the hell is everything? Instead of walls, ceilings, and bookcases, all I see is trees...and shrubs! And there's the sound of a breeze, rustling the foliage all around me.

A thought occurred to me; so I took a look around me, waiting for Rod Sterling to walk out from the underbrush, and to welcome me to the Twilight Zone. But, that couldn't happen; he's *dead*. And, if this really *is* the Twilight Zone, isn't there usually some kind of guide to show me around?

I figure that this must be a dream...a *bad* dream. Yeah, that must be it! I'm not yet fully awake, and I'm simply somehow stuck in the tail end of a dream of some sort. If I am truly still asleep, and let myself just "go with the flow," then I should wake up back in the office, getting ready to head home for the day.

So, I rested my head back on the headrest of the chair, I closed my eyes, and I started that pattern of deep, even breathing that I teach my patients, when they're having trouble sleeping; and I tell them to wait for the arms of Morpheus. I imprinted the memory of my office, and of my town, in my thoughts; and I remained in this repose for at least thirty seconds, or as long as I could possibly tolerate, under the circumstances. And then, I decided to open just one eye, and peek around me.

Crap! I'm still *here*, wherever *here* is!

This is not the easiest thing to deal with; I mean, here I was, just questioning my *beliefs*, in general. And this kind of thing certainly doesn't make a task like *that* any easier.

What am I supposed to do?

Am I supposed to sit here, and wait for Fate to play out her hand?

Maybe, I should scream for help....But, to whom? As far as I can tell, right now, *I* seem to be *it*. Sitting still is a sure way of getting no place, fast.

So, I decided to stand up, taking my cane in hand, and started walking...but, in what direction should I head? Considering my level of knowledge about this place, and in this time, it doesn't really matter much, does it? Any direction in which I happen to be facing should serve my purpose as well as any other.

The real question was whether or not I'd be able to tolerate the terrain; after all, the light was dim, and my leg has been my nemesis since I was a baby. That was funny, though; I found that I wasn't gritting my teeth with each step. Why do you think *that* is, I wondered? No pain? That cinches it; this has *got* to be a dream.

But, what if this *isn't* a dream!

No...I don't even *want* to think of the options; I've been watching too much of that Sci-Fi Network on cable, man. Beam me up, Scotty!...*That* didn't work. What now?

I'm supposed to be clever; I studied all sorts of philosophy, anthropology, and psychology over the years. I even *taught* it. And I went to graduate school in *California*; so, if there's some unorthodox explanation for this, I should have come across some explanation of it out there. All my more orthodox friends...you, know, in the East...thought that all that "touchy-feely" stuff was a lot of bull. But, here I am, trying all that voo-doo, that you do, so well, to paraphrase that song.

What's this! I don't feel scared. It seems to be working. How do you like that! Here I am, walking without the aid of my cane, and my leg doesn't ache...and, so far, nothing's come out of the bushes to devour me. And I feel *lighter*; not the usual ton of off-balance bricks I usually am.

Whatever it *is*, it can't be all bad. Maybe I should just "go with the flow," as they say. I don't seem to have much choice in this, anyway. Let's just see which way the wind blows. Like the song, maybe the answer is blowing in the wind.

So, I wet my index finger, and raised it in front of me. The wind seemed to be blowing in from the East...so I'll follow the wind to the West.

I just walked along, my cane slung over my shoulder, holding on to it in case the pain in my leg should return...but, it *didn't*! I can't be sure how long I had been walking, since, for some strange reason, my wristwatch was not there, either. That didn't matter much at the time, because I wasn't getting tired. As I trampled along, covering the uneven ground, a saying came to mind, which befit this situation: "Just when I thought I was over-the-hill, there was another hill". Hills there were aplenty, as I continued my journey in this strange territory.

Although it took some time, my eyes eventually became accustomed to the dimness of the lighting, so I was able to safely avoid many of the potential pitfalls, which presented themselves. As I contemplated the direction I would follow, I remembered an old therapeutic process, which had been used in "guided imagery" with my patients. While the individual was in a state of relaxation, I would have them develop the image of a scene, such as the one in which I found myself now, and I would ask them to turn in one direction or the other, each such instruction containing clinically significant messages.

By this method, a turn toward one's left was representative of the individual turning towards his past, and the opposite for a turn to the right, or his future. As these thoughts passed through my consciousness, I mused on my own gullibility, of falling into this line of thinking at a moment like this. Many of my friends had been educated in the more conservative realm of the East, and had laughed at some of the "antics" taught in that "touchy-feely" school *I* attended, in California.

Despite what others may have said, this line of thinking seemed so appropriate at this time. And, what's more, it seemed to genuinely express that deeper part of me, which was immersed in this place. Nobody else was here; so, that made my own choices more significant. Nobody had ever said that I *wasn't* neurotic, after all.

This was turning into a real "trip," by any definition of the word. I wondered; if this were truly a therapeutic exercise, would I be able to follow this path far enough back into my own past to come out at a point which existed *before* I got so screwed up that this kind of thing could happen to me? Whether this was the intent of this experience, my mind was replaying scenes from my past, as if on a CD; but, this time through, I was able to see clearer. As I grew older, I guess I really did gain a different slant on life.

Wait! Did I say "*slant*"? Why do you think I would use *that* word?

When I was two or three, and recently out of that cast on my left side, my mother would take me for a walk, usually to the park, which was across from our apartment house. For some reason, I always envisioned everything at a forty-five degree angle. That's kinda weird, huh? Well, no, actually. You see, I was full of piss and vinegar in those days, and my mother had a hard time to keep up with me; so, she used to put me in one of those harnesses. I even have pictures of me, when I was a baby, out there in front, leaning all the way forward, and dragging my mother behind. You know, my whole life, I've had a feeling that someone was trying to hold me back. I'd always attributed it to my own uncertainties, my own anxieties. But, maybe...maybe it's more than that. I've always believed that many of the problems we suffer in later life were actually the result of early life conditioning. If you could only whittle away the adult, and get back down to that "child," you'd be able to better understand what happened.

At around age four, there was that fall from that cement wall, on the sides of the driveway. I sprained my thigh, and had to go for treatments. I became a lot more aware of myself, and had to learn greater control over the wilder impulses of my childhood; all those things which let a kid be a kid. There were quite a few medical emergencies back then, and each played its role in shaping my future, and the way I would deal with the world. Each situation placed me at the "mercy" of the "people in white," those "angels" of mercy. But, you know, to a four year old, who may be tied to a bed, and immobilized, their treatment would not be considered angelic. Besides which, referring to them as "angels" of any sort does not offer comfort to a tormented child. Angels are associated with Heaven, you know, *death*. What I was seeking was a rapid return to my play world.

So, let's see; where does that bring us? Oh, yeh. You heard of the "Ox-Bow Incident"? Well, age five brings *me* to the infamous "fish bone" incident. In my practice, I hear a lot of people questioning how some seemingly minor incident could affect a person's whole life. I think that the focal issue here is that one is only assessing the impact of the incident at a point in one's life when one has been able to "put things into per-spective," so to speak. At age five, my mother served us some fish for supper, and, like my father, my habit was to bite, swal-low, chew...in *that* order. But, believe me, that changed quickly. Damn, I couldn't even stand the *smell* of fish for more than twenty years after *that*.

I got that sucker caught so far down in my throat that I couldn't dislodge it, no matter what I tried. I did the water things, the dry bread thing, and then I just gagged for a few minutes. The folks threw me into the family car, and drove me to the doctor's office (Oh, those were the *old* days, when doctors would see you at *any* hour). He reached down my throat with one of those pointy instruments, but couldn't get hold of the damn thing. The best he could offer was for me to just wait it out, and it would eventually dissolve on its own. Yeh; thanks for nothing. I felt that thing every time I swallowed for the next few days. Having lived in coastal areas since college, I've developed my taste for seafood; but, I'll tell you what, there's always just that momentary hesitation every time I just think about having fish.

Moving on, what other significant adventures may have played a role in my ending up here?

Gee, there's a memory that's escaped me for the past forty-five years, or so. If I close my eyes, I can still see little Georgie, and Betty Jean, out in the garage, behind the house. I believe that they were playing "doctor," and they invited me in for a consultation. Wellllllllllll...maybe I'd just better let this memory slide by, just to be safe...Hmmmmmmmmm.

I wonder how far I've gone. I haven't been paying much attention, but this path seems to be winding around, and now it's heading toward the West, or to the left.

What comes to mind is one of those processes whereby one uses imagery to examine one's own psyche, and being able to review one's past. As I continue my journey on this path, I've been able to catch glimpses of the more significant episodes of my life as I pass through them, in the process of aging. Far out! To tell you the truth, I don't really mind re-

membering the *good* times; but I can't say that there were that
many of them. There are an awful lot of things I've worked
hard over the years, placing as far back in my memory as possible.

So, heading back to the West, and moving forward with my
life, we've made it past old "fishbone," and I can remember
my dad building the home they lived in, until just this year. We
had made it out of the city when I was around three, and now I
was just entering first grade. He was building this new place
so we might be more "comfortable"; but I knew what he meant.
He was looking for a more "culturally appropriate" neighborhood for us, with people "more like *us*".

My mom had just gotten her driver's license, and was going to taxi us up to the new town each morning, so we could
start the school year in the new town. That must have been
around '51 or '52. Mom would pack my brother and I into the
Olds, and drive us as far as the building site early every morning. This was so we could get used to the neighborhood, and
the walk to school. We simply followed the other kids, and
hoped that they were headed to school. We'd walk down the
block, to that statue of George Washington on his horse, across
from Washington's Headquarters, and then down Morris Av-
enue, to the school. That was how I got to meet all those kids,
who are still my friends now, even after all these years, and all
this distance.

I was starting first grade, and my brother was starting fifth,
I think. There was no such thing as eating lunch at school in
those days. Each noontime, my brother and I would walk back
to the building site, and my mother would meet us with a bag
lunch she had made. In the beginning, we would sit in the car;
but, as the place began to grow, we'd sit on a pile of cinderblock,

then on the foundation, then on the framing, and then, finally, just as the weather was beginning to chill, we moved inside.

Looking back, those were probably among the best times of my life. We, as a family, were pretty close back then, at least my mother, brother, and I. Dad was still busy with his other work sites, and we'd see him for a few minutes, at supper.

Once we had moved into the house, those *other* memories start creeping into the picture. My doctors have always said that it was remarkable how healthy I am, considering how sick I can get. As far back as I can remember, I had some injury or infection. The problems with my leg started when I was nine months old. I always had swelling somewhere on my body, which, I later discovered, might relate to something called "angioneurotic edema," a kind of vague, generalized allergy, which can hit me at any time stress has caused my immune system to break down.

Well, that first year, my lips swelled to the point that I looked like Goldie Hawn, in that movie, <u>The First Wive's Club</u>, after she had gotten carried away with hose collagen injections. Over the years, I've had swelling all over. I can bloat internally as well as externally, and my throat can shut closed.

Hell! I knew that would open the flood-gates with unwanted memories. That problem with my leg, back when I was an infant, resulted in a slowly developing deformity over the years. By the time I had reached ten or so, we noticed that there was a bowing in my left knee, and I was referred back to the specialist, in New York, who had treated me as an infant. Then it was back and forth to New York, to the University Hospital, for varying attempts at stopping the deformity, and straightening my leg.

Each such surgical intervention resulted in me being away from home, for weeks at a time; and then I spent months alone in the house, on the mend. The worst part is that it was never very successful, and my left leg remains several inches shorter than the right, with a large bow in it, and PAIN!

But, I have to admit, with all that crap going on, there was something good that did happen. As a result of my extended periods out of school, the school system had to provide a tutor for me, in the home. Here I was, in the sixth grade, and my tutor was a high school physics teacher, Mr. R. He would come to the house twice a week, from four to five in the afternoon, just in time for The Mickey Mouse Club on television. First, we'd have milk and cookies, and then we'd watch TV. When we did focus on the schoolwork, I managed to complete most of the requirements for several grade levels in the first few months. After that, Mr. R would bring some of the math and science books from high school, and we'd see how much I was able to understand.

I was no longer totally bored. I would still be stuck on the cot, in the den, all day and night, because I couldn't climb the steps to the bedroom. However, now I had these books to work on, and to occupy my mind. It certainly did a lot for my self-confidence, if only from the little compliments he would offer now and then for the work I was doing. It helped me to develop something of an "ego," a rational self. And, by the time I was able to get up and around, and able to finally rejoin my friends at school, I found the academics to be a breeze. What I had been deprived of for all those months, was a social life. There was a matter of confidence, and social processing which had suffered.

There were many more ups and downs in my life; but, all that befell me seemed only to help to make me stronger. Not that I would always see it that way. There were plenty of times that I felt sorry for myself, like a misfit, or an anachronism. I often felt out-of-place, or out-of-time. But, even when I was at my most depressed, or at my angriest, there always appeared to be a golden beam of sunshine to break through the gloom, no matter how small it might have been.

Looking back, as I was, it became more and more evident that, even at my lowest moments, I was aware that I could exercise some measure of *control* over my own life. I know that I had often complained that I felt like a ping-pong ball, being bounced back and forth by the forces of life. But, maybe, the concept of "control" really takes the form of the *choices* we make in our lives. Maybe *that*, somehow, was the *spark* of light I was supposed to be seeking in this wilderness before me.

As this point passed through my mind, I looked up, and, in the distance, I could see the sparkle of a faint light. All else was in total darkness by now, as the day had passed into night. There was *something* out there. I adjusted my heading, and started walking in that direction, a little cautious as to what I might find. With that light as my reference point, I gradually made my way, in as straight a line as I could, toward it.

As I approached, the light became larger and larger, until, upon making it over a slight rise in the landscape, I could more clearly make out a *campfire*. As I came closer, I was able to make out images, which seemed to be gathered around this campfire, roughly in a circle of sorts. As I was just outside the very fringe of this circle, I could hear something, or someone, coming out of the darkness behind me; and, tapping me gently on the shoulder, he said, "Come on in, and join us. All are welcome here." He didn't seem to have any compunctions about entering this circle, and this encouraged me to follow his footsteps the rest of the way across this field, and into this gathering. When he found his way to a place alongside the fire, I joined him, and took a seat.

One might have expected that I would be filled with greater anxiety by all of this, being approached from the blind side like that, and then confronting a group of strangers. But, even *I* was surprised that I wasn't surprised.

For the first time, I looked around me, at the faces which were visible in the fire's glow. It was difficult seeing all the details, but I became aware of the unusual variety of garb displayed. While the group as a whole was rather large, they seemed to have been arranged in subgroups, based on some characteristic or other, whether it be their language, their clothing, or their beliefs...but I had no way of knowing just yet.

At the far end of the circle, near an opening to a cave, seemed to be the most primitive of individuals, in physical characteristics, and in function. As I listened to the conversation from that end of the gathering, I eventually learned that this primitive was named "Mog". He was anthropoid, alright; but there was a great deal of facial and body hair, his posture was more like that of the great apes, and he didn't appear to be able to form "words," as I would be able to understand them. He was dressed in hides and skins, roughly pieced together; and, in his hand, he held some kind of stone figure, at which he would chip, from time to time, bringing out a female form from the hard and unforgiving material.

I hadn't realized it before this very moment, but language didn't seem to be a problem for me. Although this Mog didn't seem capable of rational speech, I seemed to be able to understand what he was trying to convey. As a matter of fact, while I recognized a number of different tongues being spoken, I had no difficulty understanding any of them. Mog's gestures and grunts were as clear to me as the gentleman at my side, speaking the finest English.

There appeared to be lively conversations going on within the smaller groupings, as well as within the circle as a whole; but, as I approached, a quiet began to drift through the crowd. A young woman approached, and offered me a cup, from which smoke gently rose. I was querulous, but she gestured for me to drink. I lifted it to my lips, and slowly poured a little into my mouth.

"Hmmmmmmmm....Sweet....Good!" I sat back, and looked more closely at this object she had handed me. From some of the texts I had read, I recognized this as a form of "chalice". And the beverage in it was a mild, herbal, fruity beverage, like some sort of mulled wine, but with the taste of honey. I looked about me again, feeling quite entertained by what I saw. And then, without thinking, I must have said something like, "Jesus, this is quite a group, isn't it?"

From my right, a gentle figure, wearing a crown of thorns, and displaying a cherubic smile, leaned forward, and answered, "Why, yes it is, isn't it? I'm glad that you could join us."

While his expression was somehow comforting, I was somewhat taken aback by his approach. All I could muster was, "Excuse me?"

He smiled again, and then he drew back and laughed out loud to himself. I felt uncomfortable now; so I asked, "And what's so funny?"

"Oh, I'm sorry. You asked me a question, and I was just offering my response."

"Wait a minute here; did I miss something?" Then I had to think to myself, "Is he saying what I think he's saying?" But I must have said this out loud, unwittingly, because this individual again smiled broadly, and commented, "I'm very sorry, but it hadn't occurred to me that you might have been unaware."

"Unaware of *what*?" I was becoming a bit frustrated by this time. After all, nobody likes to be laughed at. And, besides, I wasn't sure that he was saying what I *thought* he was saying. Maybe people had been right; maybe, if you're around delusional people all day in your work, you may somehow pick it up. Maybe I had missed something along the way.

Noticing my discomfort, he smiled, leaned forward, placed a gentle hand on my shoulder, and offered his apologies, adding, "You'll have to excuse us. You see, we, here, are not as affected by these kinds of uncertainties, and these *mundane* emotions, as you are. And, for that reason, I guess we weren't attuned to where you were at. You will have to forgive us."

"What the hell are you calling *mundane*?...Are you calling me 'common,' or something!" I was starting to get steamed, which is only a short trip to travel from frustrated. I thought that I'd show him "mundane," with each hairy knuckle on my fist.

But, he must have somehow read what I was thinking, for he quietly stood, stretched his arms out to the rest of the gathering, to gain their attention, and pleaded, "Excuse me, my brothers and sisters; but I fear we may have sorely aggrieved this poor pilgrim. Let us respect his confusion."

I felt like President Reagan when I jumped in with, "There you go *again*. Just what the hell is this *pilgrim* stuff! What are you calling me? Is this supposed to be Canterbury Tales, or something"!

"Be assured, my friend, that we are all of one mind". Turning to the others, he added, "My friends, this poor fellow appears to be vexed with the human frailties, which most of us have long since lost touch with".

Again, with the 'human frailties'. "So, are *you* above that sort of thing, for cryin' out loud!"

He was having some trouble quieting my feelings. "I apologize for the apparent insensitivity with which we handled your arrival. You must know that it has been a while since we have been approached thusly by a mortal".

"*Mortal*!...Wait a minute...What're you saying? I don't think I like the direction this is taking!" Geez...If this *isn't* just a dream...I don't even want to think of the alternatives...Why would he call me a *mortal*? "But, I can *feel* things; and my *senses* are still intact!" Dare I even broach the subject?

There was no need for me to say anything further, as the members of the groups appeared to sit back, and to relax. The gentleman at my side, with whom I had been conversing, stepped forward from the group. He was wearing a gown of simple cloth, had sandals on his feet, and a reddish beard.

"Let me introduce myself," and he bowed. "I am called *Jesus*, of Nazareth. And, because it was I that spoke first, in response to your query, does not make of me the *leader* of this group. We are all of one here, as are *you*, now that you have joined our little journey."

Whoa! I quickly made amends for that "Jesus" remark before, and explained that it had surfaced out of my confusion of the moment. It was just something that us 'humans' tend to say in those situations. I suddenly remembered all that Old Testament stuff about using the Lord's name in vain, and the wrath of God. Oy! I was in for it now.

"Hey! I didn't get on your bad side, did I? I mean, have a heart; after all, I'm only *human*...Or, should I say it, 'I'm *only* human'?" Stop me, someone...I'm just forcing my foot deeper in my mouth!

"No need exists for your apologies. As a matter of fact, it would be my guess that *we* must have a few expressions, which we would use in similar situations. However, I'm not certain that humans would be capable of comprehending their significance, as they may make reference to things of which you are, as yet, unaware. Please, be at peace. We are not so easily swayed as may have been suggested in some of the books you have read". This said, he turned to others across the fire, and he asked, "What say you? Were the words of the mortals to be considered accurate in describing our fickle nature?"

A large gentleman, in robes of heavy cloth, carrying a large chalice in hand, rose, and faced his questioner. "I fear that I was not fully understood in *my* day. Perhaps it was that the mortals had such a need for a strong and caring paternal figure, that could be capable of managing their motives". He then turned directly toward me. "I'm sorry. May I introduce my humble self. The Greeks knew me as Zeus. And may I introduce some of the members of my family, including this lovely young thing, Hera, my wife. And these are my children."

I must have appeared to be dumb-founded, as the individual to my side reached up, and gently closed my mouth for me, which had been agape in disbelief. I could not be sure exactly what it was that I was hearing. Feeling that I had nothing further to lose by venturing forth, I asked, "Are you suggesting, then, that I'mmmmm.....Let's see, how may I put this so I don't sign my own commitment papers?...Are you suggesting that I may be in the midst of...how to put this...the DEITIES"?!

"We never really think of ourselves quite in *that* way, here. That which the mortals, and the animals, hold and believe about us is not the same as that which we each hold about ourselves."

"Huh!...Animals?...Are you saying that *animals* have deities, too"?

"Why does that surprise you? Wasn't it your own Darwin who tried to make it clear that the homo sapien was simply one of the numerous species which lay within the animal kingdom? It is, of course, also true that Darwin tended to place Man head and shoulders above the rest...but, Man has always had that ego problem, hasn't he"?

Another figure rose. "I remember when that chimpanzee, down there in, what was that place...Nevada...started using human sign language; didn't that make them stop and think"?

"But there are always those literalists, who keep pounding those books they carry with them, and keep exalting the human as being the king of all the beasts. And, in Atlanta, Georgia, in that primate laboratory, where they trained all those apes to use computerized boards to make complete sentences, there were always other humans ready to seek an alternate explanation, which might better allow them to feel that they maintained their supremacy on the hierarchy of the phylogenetic ladder."

I was beginning to feel overwhelmed by all of this. All I could do was to slump down in my seat, and hang my head in my hands, and try to make some sense of this all. "This has been so-o-o-o much to digest, in such a short time. But, to be honest, it really isn't much more than I've already let myself think on my own, from time to time. At certain times, like, especially, around election times, I had had to wonder how Mankind had ever gotten so screwed up. There had been so much written about deities, with each following another path in its search of what to believe in. I had often come to the question, "What is the *purpose* of religion?" There was never any *one* satisfactory answer".

I took another sip from that cup given to me earlier, and thought for a second. "I can remember a time, back, when I was in graduate school, and searching for the most fitting topic for my doctoral dissertation; I awoke one night, and the word "**CERTAINTY**" stood out like a beacon, in my mind. I was awake just enough to walk to the hall closet, open the door, and use the pen and pad I generally kept there for just such moments, and quickly scribbled down my ideas. When I awoke, and after performing my morning ablutions in the bathroom, I made my usual stop to check the closet. I could hardly make out the chicken-scratchings I found there; but I made out that one word, "certainty".

"And so, I went to the dictionary, and I looked the word up. It described a search for a state of being "fixed" or "settled"; the "inevitable"; reliable and dependable, and, the most interesting of all, something *definite, but unnamed!*

"I could see that the definition of "uncertainty" could have easily represented any number of Man's images of himself. One is occupied by the image of the first humanoid creatures; or, if you will, of Adam and Eve, in the Garden of Eden. *That*, my friend, *had* to be the definition of uncertainty, in *all* of its possible meanings.

"The same day I handed in my doctoral dissertation, I remember picking up a book in the university bookstore, which totally blew me away. Over the years, I must have lost ten copies to people that I had lent it to; but, then again, I had purchased a dozen copies, once I realized the magic of this book. It was one of the first books to be published by the Playboy Press, in 1975. The title was THE RAPE OF THE A.P.E., by Allen Sherman, the humorist. A.P.E. stood for "the American Puritan Ethic". In the book, Allan Sherman introduces his protagonist, Sap, which is short for "sapien", who is described as he wanders aimlessly through his early existence on Earth, with an infantile glee at everything the world presents to him for his pleasure.

"Although our boy Sap enjoys his existence, he eventually finds that there may be something which is missing, something which might help him enjoy his life even more. This started his search for that magical ingredient which would increase the value of his life, and which might offer it greater meaning and purpose. The rest of the story, I'm sure you can guess."

With this, a gentleman, in Greek garb, rose, and asked that I not doubt the things I am about to experience, but to wait until I may have more information on which to base my opinion. "I realize that all of this is quite a bit to grasp right off. But, for the moment, I ask for nothing more than you simply *accept* it for what it is.

"I am no fool, and realize that this is the very thing which all "rational" men may challenge most, the seemingly blind acceptance of something which one cannot completely comprehend. But, at least in this case, you are not completely alone; *we* are here, within your senses, and we are asking at least for you to accept *us*, at least on an equal footing. Is this too much to ask from a fellow pilgrim as ourselves?"

Chapter Three

It has always been difficult for humans to be able to accept anything simply *on blind faith*, if you will; but Mankind has been more accepting of that which is presented to his senses. For *me*, in the present situation, to actively accept that which assailed my senses, was not exceptionally difficult. But, to accept these characters as "deities"...*that* might prove to be a different story.

And, therein lies the "paradox of man," from the beginnings of time itself. As I viewed the more primitive characters at the fire, I could somehow comprehend some of the confusion which had to be a natural part of their day. They believed in those Venus figures...yeh, I knew what they were; I'd read about them in anthropology class...because that, at least, was "real" for them. It was tangible. One could imagine the intense confusion of their setting out from the cave each day, challenged by everything in their environment, and, to a large degree, completely defenseless against much of it.

When I look at Mog, for instance, I am looking at Mankind in his infancy. One may compare the evolution of Man, in terms of culture, the same way one might look at a newborn infant. In his origins, he is totally helpless, at the mercy of the world around him. Mankind, in its infancy, had to be weak of both mind and body, until that magical ingredient, "civilization," was added to the formula. Of course, with the addition of civilization, one had acquired the ability to recognize that Man was also *morally* weak.

Man set out crawling into the world, his progress frustrated at every move. Any directions he might receive would be totally dependent on his family, made up of others who had successfully traveled that path before him. Here, man received direction, as well as protection, until he had gained the skills necessary to tackle the world on his own. And this was necessary, for the preservation of the species, for the betterment of Mankind as a whole. If he should remain, and, for some reason, mate only with the limited resources available to him, there would be a devastating contamination of the "gene pool," which could only weaken the species even further. The process of "diversity," the variation of the genetics in breeding outside of one's immediate group, would help to deplete the recessive genes, and to incorporate strengths into the offspring.

The world serves as a parent to man, offering succor and guidance, through experience and reinforcement. Since life was generally harsh, it was evident that only the stronger, or smarter, or faster might survive. Man may have perceived himself simply as a pimple on the butt of the physical world, miniscule, in comparison to the grandeur which presented itself to his senses each day. And, in part as a result of this weakness, Man had learned to *question everything*. He was, as yet, too vulnerable to have been able to safely accept *anything* at face value. Mankind was but an infant in the wilderness, seeking to gain in skills with every breath he took. His judgment was conceived of as being seriously flawed, as it was based on a minimum of experience in this world.

Each step which he took was toward something new, perhaps performed with the purpose of finding food or shelter; and each such step served to make him more aware of just how ignorant and insignificant he actually was. One must remember that the earliest man survived on food gathering, and was dependent on whatever the world could lay at his feet. Whatever he ate was presented to him in its purest form, unworked and raw. Whatever meat he might enjoy was gained by sharing the kill by some other animal, and was eaten raw. Man learned about hunting by observing those animals who were most successful at it; and then he added whatever technology he was able to create, in an effort at creating those weapons the other animals possessed naturally. The sharpened stones and bone became the claws and the teeth, which wounded the prey. The projectiles he eventually designed made up for his lack of swiftness afoot.

Man's great advantage over the other animals was that he could learn and adapt, and develop tools and skills which would extend his potential beyond the mere limits of his physical body. Initially, this resulted in a change in Man's diet from seeds, plants, roots, fruits, and vegetables, which were mostly carbohydrates, to fish and small animals, which were protein. As long as he depended mostly on the carbohydrates, he would have energy; but he would have to replenish his supply frequently, as these carbohydrates had short-term effects. This diet also limited Man as to the size to which he could grow, since the body requires protein to build muscle and sinew.

And with the ability to take advantage of the larger animals for food, he also developed a need for *cooperation*, a process in which the stronger, and more skilled of men, would earn the rights to the greater spoils. Even if an individual were able to bring down a larger beast, he had no way of transporting it alone, and the greater part of it might spoil before he could get to it. This mutual dependency led to the development of *trust* among people, and mutual protection; otherwise, one might just wait for another to make a kill, and then steal it from him. But now, one was dealing with the well-being of a family unit, or a living group, all supported by this hunt.

Man's survival was also dependent on the season, and on the resources of each particular area. As long as man simply gathered food as he found it, he was forced into a nomadic lifestyle, moving with the season. However, with time, he discovered that there were fertile regions in the river valleys, and in the deltas formed by the water. At these locations, there was a supply of life-giving water, a prevalence and diversity of vegetation, a source of fish, and a means of transportation. By learning to cultivate, or bring certain plants closer to the water source and fertile ground, Man was able to create "roots" for himself. Residences became more permanent, and the interaction of the people became formalized. Thus developed the *institutions of civilization*, or what would eventually be called "culture". And one of the institutions of any culture is "religion".

For the first time in the evolution of Man, he developed the ability to possess *excess*, stores of various food types, which could be put aside for times of need. By lessening the stress on him for perpetual subsistence living, Man could actually take into consideration the things that he did, or plan a better way of doing it...He could *think about thinking*. Life became more than simply a struggle to survive, or to subsist. He could question why everything was as it was. He could go beyond the phenomenon of existence itself, and he could question the *purpose*, or the *meaning*, which might stand behind each thing...including himself.

All that existed had to come from *someplace*...and it might be *headed* someplace. While, in his journey through this world, man was able to view, and to map, the path that things took through the world, he was still unable to gain a perspective on its *source*, or starting point, or its end-point.

Once Man was able to distance himself from the actual effort it took for daily survival, and to view *things* from a different perspective, a concept arose that there might be a power at work, which could be a great deal more powerful than he. Perhaps this concept arose from a reverence within a tribe, or clan, for those who possessed certain prized attributes or skills, which were important to the survival of the group. It is not surprising that one develops a form of reverence, or *fear*, for anyone who holds the power of *your* life in his hands.

I am reminded of a story told by comedian, Mel Brooks, who, as the Two-Thousand Year Old Man, was interviewed by Carl Reiner. Asked if he could recall the earliest form of deity, Mel Brooks said, "Sure. There was Bernie". What was so different about Bernie? Well, if you just looked at him cross-eyed, he'd reach out, and rip the nose right off of your face. Everyone worshipped him, because they were afraid of him.

Then, one day, while Bernie was standing outside the cave during a thunderstorm, a bolt of lightning lit up the sky. It shot out of the clouds, and toasted Bernie, right there on the spot. Asked how they had developed a belief in something beyond Bernie, Mel Brooks said, "Gevault!"...Asked who this deity was, Mel Brooks said that, after seeing the lightning hit Bernie, they looked at each other and said, "Gevault!...There's something bigger than Bernie!" Following this instant barbeque, be it at poor Bernie's expense, there developed an instant respect for this new-found force. One simply does not question power like that.

Such a show of power would be paralyzing; and, while one may not readily be able to uncover the source of that power, one would feel a need to accept a belief in a higher power...perhaps on faith alone. To question this force once it had been witnessed, and even if its source remained unseen, would thereafter be considered a "sin," a willful break with some moral or religious law. It would be like challenging something which had proven itself to be "all-powerful".

And so, what, you may ask, exactly is the "paradox"?

First, if one should happen to lack the blind faith which is necessary to accept that an "all-powerful" entity exists, then one is said to have committed the most heinous of sins.

On the other hand, if one should drop any pretense of doubt and actually start accepting openly the realities of the Earthly world, as well as the possibilities of a *next* world, then one has violated one of the prime rules taught by those with a survival mentality; and one has again sinned.

The beauty of this type of thinking is that it is so beautifully circular, closed, and unbeatable. Is there no wonder that so many have attempted to work out the apparent flaws in such a system? If one were to examine the totality of Man's thinking, starting in the Stone Age, and following right through to the present, one would have to see that Mankind has taken what started out as a reasonable idea, and they have somehow contaminated it with the very poison that is the sole creation of Man.

But, that is not the only paradox of Man, you understand. As if reading my thoughts, another took the floor.

"From the very beginnings of Man, in his deepest and darkest past, in those days when Man first stood upright, and raised his knuckles off the ground, Man became a *creature of cus-*

tom. He developed proscribed modes of functioning, which he thereafter staunchly defended with all his strength. It is Mankind's will to create diverse habits, on which he may fall for a sense of support, at those times of greatest stress.

"He is equally discomforted by that which is handed to him by Nature. He cannot accept things in their original form, and then he manipulates it, as a way of further controlling his natural instincts, which he has never trusted. He takes that which is given, and appears to respond to some unseen force, which urges him to place his personal mark on each thing, whatever it may be. If that world, into which Man is born, is perceived as being in any way lacking, or performs in any way which is unsatisfactory to his tastes, then he will invariably seek to make appropriate alterations in that situation. And, if for some reason, he finds that it is not possible for him to directly manipulate that reality, he will, at the very least, *daydream* an alternate reality, one in which the situation has become more amenable to his wants and needs. I believe that this is one of the points which was presented by your writer, Carlos Castaneda, when he described "A Separate Reality"."

This spoken, I see another rise, among those identified as the Egyptian gods, and introduced herself as Isis. "Since his very beginnings as a thinking being, Man has always felt that there was importance to his making some estimate of the origins of what he knew as "civilized" man. I believe that it was as late as the Seventeenth Century that Archbishop Usher, of the Anglican Church, using the Old Testament as his reference, placed the *exact* date of creation at 4004 B.C."

At this point, the discussion around the camp was becoming quite animated, with diverse reactions from all sides. Yet, there seemed to be a complete absence of harsh recriminations, or outbursts of violence, even with the most emotional of differences.

This, then, would appear to be what the tenor of this gathering would become, as we were to investigate the origins of Man, and his beliefs, as it would be actively debated among those who were actually the subject of that worship. An interesting perspective, to be sure. How often is one afforded the opportunity of not only debating the pros and cons of a situation in which one was intimately involved, but to be able to defend oneself, without some form of human aggression being involved?

And Isis continued. "This estimate, then, offered up by the noble Archbishop, may be intriguing indeed, especially in light of later carbon dating of mammalian fossils at about one hundred million years. And the origins of the humanoid mammals has been similarly dated to about five hundred thousand years in the past.

"But all this debate may be for naught; and, in fact, appears little more than intellectual drivel. The earliest material records of Man's *history* have only existed, in some form of readable evidence or other, for the past five or six thousand years. Prior to this, all estimate had to be estimated from artifacts which Man may have left behind. It is difficult to make estimates and judgments from the least chard or artifacts as were left by those, such as our partner there, Mog."

A gentleman approached, wearing a toga, with the material elegantly draped over his arm. I had recognized him as from the Greek contingent, from books I had read.

"The problem afforded by the concept of *death* may be offered as a starting point for the study of...yea, the *need* for...a system of philosophy".

"This was profound, indeed," I thought to myself. Man is usually too caught up in his daily functioning to reflect on it. It is only when there is cause to be halted in one's efforts that one takes the time for looking back; and *that*, death certainly serves.

"Some of the oldest of Man's shared beliefs possess a dual focus. First, they examine the direction of *this* life. Second, they take a view of how this life might play out should one actually be capable of achieving those goals he has set for the next life".

There arose some commotion, as this point was being aired. It appears that there were those among this gathering that held the belief that one's experience on this Earth represents the sum total of all existence for Man, and that looking beyond this was pure folly. That which one could see and feel was all that truly existed. Once this experience on Earth was completed, one became only fodder for further generations. So, I asked, "Do you then say that all one can believe is that which one senses? Is that so?"

This Greek thought on this for a moment, and then said, "That is what some believe; however, if one examines even the most primitive of ancient cultures, one would find evidence of some further belief, in their burial practices. First, the fact of a burial tells of some respect for that life. And then, the manner in which one is buried often suggests that there exists a view of some form of existence beyond this one".

Again, there is greater commotion, as varying schools of thought and belief tangle amongst themselves on this issue.

"What proof, you ask,"? he responded rhetorically to the unstated question. "On all points of this globe, those who have deceased have been found interred with some preparation, rather than simply being left to the elements, or to the beasts of the night. Furthermore, they were buried along with objects which had been familiar to their style of life, such as household tools and implements, some aesthetic artifacts, and even foodstuffs, as if to fuel them on their longest journey. Would it not be possible to interpret this behavior as preparing the individual for service in the next life?

"There is yet further proof of this belief in "life after life". I suggest that these primitives have buried their departed in a variety of positions other than a simple reclining posture. The most suggestive of these postures is with the body placed on its side, with its knees drawn up to its chest, its arms pulled in to its sides, and the hands placed across the chest. One, I think, would readily recognize this as the "fetal position," which signifies the posture of the unborn fetus, while it remains inside the body of the mother. This very practice might lead one to believe that these same "primitives" believed so much in an "after-life" that the body of the deceased would be prepared for its "rebirth" in the next life.

"The very fact that these cultures would seek such means of preserving the physical remains in some way speaks to the belief that there had to be some consideration of "*time*," a measure of which could be so vast that only some miniscule portion of it would be represented by Man's activities on Earth.

"And burial practices revealed quite a bit about the culture in which they were practiced, as well as giving clues as to the underlying philosophy of that people. There are yet, even today, societies which exist in the Modern Stone Age; peoples who have been protected from "modernization" by the extremes of their location. There are those who have only recently been brought into the Twentieth, or Twenty-First Century, who, as yet, cling tenaciously to the beliefs of their past, and to the traditions which accompany them. It would seem that any culture, placed under enough stress as to impede effective decision-making, may regress to that stage of development in their existence, which held the most secure answers for them. Is this not very much like that doctor, what's his name...Freud...Is this not what he had stated about the individual who might find himself under such overwhelming stress?"

All of this had set the group abuzz with excitement, each generation of deity sharing some piece of its knowledge which it possessed, seeking to make of it a "whole". At the far end of the gathering, one could even sight Mog, dancing around the fire, raising that damn leg bone of his ancestors, that he carried around with him, and grunting something as he danced. One of the characters beside him commented, "Oh, well. I guess that his way is as good as any other, huh? It has served Mankind for the thousands, or millions, of years before Man became "*civilized*". From what has been spoken to now, one might consider civilization of the species as connoted by the discovery of greater means of destruction, which may be made with less effort on his part. I would guess that having one's head lopped off could leave him just as dead as the man who succumbs to a "weapon of mass destruction," don't you think?

"The first of the hominids, meaning the two-legged mammals, appear to have evolved within the Pleistocene Period of history, *if* you believe in evolution, that is. At this point in the development of Man, there were not yet any real tools for Man to shape his world. However, there was the first of a long line of evolutionary improvements to the organism itself; and *that* would be the hand, with an opposable thumb. It was this development which allowed Man to better manipulate his environment, offering him greater flexibility, less dependence on the climbing of trees for defense, and better able to walk without dragging his knuckles on the ground.

"Of these hominids, the first to be classified by the term, *homo sapien*, or "true man," may have been the Cro-Magnon, who arrived about fifty thousand years ago. I am not talking of the first *homo erectus*, who would have walked on two legs; but the first of the more modern man. Cro-Magnon seems to have dabbled in the representational arts, in the form of scratchings, or carvings, on the walls of his caves, and on the sides of the hills in which he lived. Archaeologists have also found chards of stone with markings on them, suggesting a similar art. It is through this representational art that one may estimate the beginnings of some form of religious thought.

"The earliest of such practices seems to have dealt with those aspects of daily life which were of greatest significance, such as one found in the gathering of food, for sustenance. An examination of this representational art could suggest a form of *magical thinking*, which would be practiced to assist Man in his search for food, and in hunting the food that he needed.

"The earliest of the cave renderings, which have been found by modern man, express an apparent exaggeration in gender differences, noted in the size of the female breasts and hips. This may well be symbolic of their reputation as the "givers of life". The masculine figures, on the other hand, illustrate an exaggeration of other appendages of the body, representing his importance as the "hunter". The overall impression one might gain from these signs is that the earliest cultures practiced a *cult of fertility*, evolving around these very factors of life. One may note that the word "culture" starts with the first four letters, of "cult". As such, both art and religion were represented in the singular form, and both expressed in the service of human survival."

Next to rise was an ancient, of the Fertile Crescent, Mesopotamia, the lands between the Tigris and the Euphrates Rivers. It would be of interest to hear *his* perspective on all of this, as he represented the area of the Earth in which modern Man is believed to have sprung.

"'Tis said that what we now hold as being modern civilization had its roots in the valley from which I have descended. If my memory holds true, that which were the first, which we might call "villages," were beginning to evolve around the year 4000 B.C. There developed a *system* of small congregates, which joined for the purposes of economy and security. Aggregating thusly, Man was better able to transmit those tenets of culture which were to assist his survival, both physically and socially. With the developments in technology, time was available through the day to perform tasks other than pure hand-to-mouth labors. Man started to weave cloth from the fiber of vegetation, which he would beat on the rocks, wash in the river, and dry in the sun; but, later, with greater success in hunting and trapping, he learned to make clothing from the hair and hide of the animals, which, by this time, he had domesticated. This, then, prepared him for greater variations in the weather, and allowed him to live in more diverse climatic zones.

"This form of congregate living was able to make greater use of those materials which were needed for the survival of the species, and also allowed for the advances in technology, enabling him to produce more than would be required for his *immediate* needs. Man was now sharing the burden of labor with his brethren, offering a portion of his meal back to the Earth, as a form of "toast," a giving of thanks to the *ultimate provider* for these resources. In any such subsistence economic system, any such 'toast" could be interpreted as a form of "sacrifice," which may have preceded the ceremonial sacrifice of animals, or even humans. This process could be considered as Man giving up something of value as a sign of appreciation for the resources the Earth gave to Mankind. Such practice was common in many areas of the Middle East, but could also be found in the Wei Valley, and in Hoang Ho, in China, then later being found prevalent in the New World, in areas of Peru and Mexico."

I was beginning to piece together some commonalities between the evolution of survival tactics, meaning "economy," and the development of what would become religious thought. Both of these, taken together, seemed to make up the bulk of what we had been discussing as "culture". From what had been presented, it would appear that the closer Man would be tied to the land for his survival, the more we found the gods to be specific to certain immediate needs, such as for food, for clothing, or for shelter. But I had to ask, "How, then, could all of these diverse beliefs, evolved at points throughout the Earth, end up becoming so similar in their basics?"

Among the Asian contingent, one dressed in furs, with oriental features, and possibly a Mongol, or a Tartar, rose to this question. "There are legends abounding of the nomad populations, who would wander the Earth, seeking to meet their needs for subsistence. They followed the herds, and the weather, which could most suitably meet their survival needs. These were not agrarian peoples, and they had to travel to where the pickings were adequate.

"They would arrive at some destination, and would mingle with those of local origins, passively absorbing that which served them best. Other, more aggressive peoples, would invade those lands which held plenty, taking for themselves what they could; and they might eventually become the dominators of the local peoples. The resultant cultural milieu might well depend on such factors as that culture which had been the older, which had best developed their survival to the land which supported them. While the conqueror may well be the stronger, in terms of physical might, it would be those with the greater adaptability which would dominate economically and culturally. A new breed of thinking would develop as one culture would impose its strengths on the other in this way.

"From this blending of cultural processes grew a leadership, which was made up of priest-kings, who wielded power which was absolute. They were to be perceived by the people as possessing both lay and religious origins. Their ministerings were transmitted to the people through a privileged class, made up of nobles and priests."

And then, looking around him, he stated, "I gladly surrender the floor to Martin Luther".

" 'Tis certain that this reflects much on that which is present in the structure of the Roman Catholic Church, even today. The Church served as the lord of the manor for its estates and lands, following feudal principles. They owned the land, and they would gather the wealth of the land into their storehouses. Of that which was thus collected and stored, any amount which may have exceeded the immediate needs of the Church was sufficient to support an entirely new class of citizen. This new group was made up of administrators, engineers, and scientist-priests, who did not earn their own living directly from their toil in the earth.

"It was at this point that *taxation* evolved as acceptable practice, and became a part of the natural flow of life. The Church had developed an interpretation of these economics as a way of stating that taxation could be the means by which the common man, the non-landholder, could repay to the soil some portion that had been given to Man, for his own survival, in a similar way as the "toast" had been explained, earlier. The toast, however, could be interpreted as a symbolic gesture, while taxation was an economic *reality*, in the absence of ceremony, or religious rites."

"From this, then," offered John Calvin, "there developed a "merchant class," a group of people who found themselves to be free from a slavery to the land, as had been the peasants for generations. These people were free to travel between areas which offered diversity from the land, or from their industry. They were able to barter with the surpluses they found in their own communities, in return for products available elsewhere, which may have been absent from their own.

"Yet, this travel served more than just the trade of merchandise and produce; it also enabled a "trade in ideas". While early European life had been so very *segmented* by geography, this new trade allowed for peoples of diverse ideas and beliefs to gain common elements, on which they could bond with other communities, and thus enlarging and strengthening the sense of "membership," which offered security. Differing ideas and beliefs could be voiced, could propagate, and thus, could eventually coexist."

Mankind had not naturally coexisted. To this point in the history of Man, one found ignorance of the beliefs and practices among men as a source for hostilities. Cooperation among the peoples, in the name of economy, then, evolved from this form of melding of communities, especially along the more fertile river valleys, which were better able to support human and plant life on a year-round basis. If the people did not have to follow the weather, or follow the herds, there could then be a greater permanence of residence, and economy. Mankind

learned the technology for processing foodstuffs, and for preservation and storage, so he could use his produce throughout
the year, as well as in times of difficulty.

However, this economic breakthrough had its shortcom-
ings as well; for, possessing such a source of wealth, it became
easy target for other cultures, which had not yet evolved to this
point. This group expressed its force against other men, instead of tilling in the soil. Its harvest came from the pockets of
others. And, as a result, there developed another group of
people, a "warrior class," who fed off the spoils of conquest.
They were motivated the same as the rest of Mankind; failure
meant starvation. While they may have held superiority in
physical strength, they eventually blended into the cultures
which they had conquered, and the distinction between the
groups began to blur. Those ideas which fostered the greatest
productivity, would be those which survived the years.

As I expressed these thoughts, I noticed that many about
the campfire would nod in agreement, from the Hittite lord,
from Asia Minor, to the Phoenician leader of the Mediterranean. But, I was still confused, and expressed it; "How the
heck does all this complicated material get passed on, I mean,
from culture to culture, and from generation to generation?
There's just so much room for distortion. When I was a kid,
we used to play this game at parties; I think it was called "tele-
graph". What we'd do is to sit in a circle, or in a long chain,
next to each other. There were a variety of famous sayings,
typed, and deposited in a hat. The person at the end of the line
would select one piece of paper from the hat, read the note
silently to himself, and then he would have to whisper it to the
person next to him. Each, in turn, then whispered the message, until it had made the full circuit, around the room. The
last person's job was to stand, and to state, out loud, the mes-

sage which he had heard. This final message frequently held little, if any, similarity to that which had been first read. So, with this culture thing, we're dealing with *all* of Mankind...It *had* to be even more confusing. And, who could ever attest for what the *original* message could have been, anyway!"

Next to me was a man, with a flowing white beard, and wearing a long robe, made of coarse material. The man, who had introduced himself earlier, as Jesus, said, "Moses? Why don't you see if you can clear things up for our fellow traveler; this one's just up your alley."

"Thanks, J.C. Hmmmmm....Well, young fella, let's see if I can put this so's you could understand...," and he paused to think for a moment.

"Well, I'm guessing that you're about the age where you'd join your folks, on a Saturday night, in front of the television, in those days *before* they employed censors. There was this program on, back then...Oh, what the heck was it?...Oh, yeh. The Ed Sullivan Show. One of his frequent guests used to be this story-teller, a guy named Myron Cohn. The audience just *loved* him. But, you know; if you want to hear some really great stories, you gotta hear some of those told by Abraham, Isaac, Jacob, and the rest of the Old Gang.

"Those were the guys who put together the Old Testament. It was made up of a large collection of stories, chronicling the history of the Jewish people. It had been gathered over the generations, from diverse and widely scattered peoples. In its original form, it was conceived as an effort at presenting the actual and exact word of God, but *as it was communicated to Man*, in the form of the "Revelations," and handed down from God to some of his Chosen People. Say, you think *you* got problems with publishers! Let me tell you; just try selling a book that's touted to be the "Word of God". That, boychick, is quite a feat.

"It turns out to be a fairly accurate historical document, at least as far as any document which has been collected, and edited, by different peoples, at different times in the process of life. Hey, remember; they didn't have the benefit of Webster's Dictionary, or the Encyclopedia Britannica, you know! They were pretty simple people back then. They had limited knowledge about the world in general. I guess you'd have to say that the Old Testament is an example of the *conventional wisdom* of the day."

"All that most of the people in this world ever get to see is *chaos*; and, frequently, history finds that Jewish people tend to get caught in the middle. How did *that* all start?"

Again, Moses paused to contemplate. "The peoples, who have become known as the Jews, are derived from nomadic Arabs, the Semites. Tradition tells us that these peoples came down from the land of Ur, in search of a better life in the western hills, and the lands around the Negeb. As I had previously mentioned, they were a simple people; they lacked the kinds of skills which might have been more common among those who resided in villages. Among them, there was no recognized form of aristocracy, since they had never considered "owning" land; after all, they were nomads, and the land was a gift from God, for *all* the peoples. However, the one thing which they *did* bring with them, was "monotheism," the belief in a singular, all-powerful God."

"That's no explanation! What led to the differences? Why were there so many misunderstandings?"

"Well, between the years 933 B.C. and 722 B.C., the Northern Tribes made the decision that they were going to separate from the rest, and it was they who formed the Kingdom of

Israel. To the south, the remainder of these people settled in the lands near Jerusalem, and formed the Kingdom of Judah. Separately, they only reigned briefly, since Israel fell to Assyria in 722 B.C., while the Kingdom of Judah was absorbed by Babylonia by the year 586 B.C.

"But...and here's the point...while the Jewish peoples had been defeated in battle, they were never fully absorbed by their conquerors. They were fiercely resistant, as a culture, and as a people. As a result of this, it was King Nebuchdrezzer who made the decision to annihilate them, and to remove them as a nuisance under his reign."

"If they had, in fact, been annihilated, then how come they're still out there? I'm sure there are plenty of people in the Middle East right now who would like an answer to that."

"If you'll remember, I *did say* that these were a *resistant* people, didn't I? Each and every effort, which has been made to dilute their influence on the world, has been unsuccessful. They are held together by a strong set of beliefs, as part of a very strong and enduring faith. From experiences of the past, it would seem that every time they are pushed, or persecuted, the harder they resist.

"In their infancy as a people, their God, that fellow over there, the one with that big grin on His face, Jehovah, He was only a tribal god, who would have been familiar to only a handful of the Jews. It wasn't until...What was it? ...Oh, yeh...the Book of Isaiah, around the year 586 A.D., that Jehovah became the *universal figure* He is today."

"So, why was this such a "tough sell"? Why was it so slow in growing?"

Again, Moses took a moment to gather his thoughts. "God, and all that He stands for, and all that He represents to the people...these are things which are so far removed from the human condition that they could never be experienced and known by the mere mortal. Mortals would possess no means for being able to describe these forces in human terms. As such, there is no way in which any mortal could truly *"know"* God.

"That's a pretty heavy message for such a simple people to grasp. For example, take a look at Mog, down there; it is a far easier task to ask those who are less cognitively sophisticated to believe in something which they can see and hear, meaning, to them, that it would be something which they could manipulate and affect, in some way. But the belief of the Jews possessed no statues, and no sacrifices, and no dances in their prayer. It was much too abstract a conception for many of the primitives to accept".

This, too, stirred a great deal of diverse sentiment around the campfire. There were the many, of the ancient schools of thought, who demanded something more concrete on which to focus their beliefs; but, then again, there were those who believed that the more abstract representations of the deity would make a better fit into the routine of daily life.

The dividing line between these schools of belief was not on the basis of antiquity of the peoples alone, with the more ancient peoples demanding the more concrete god-figures. It is true that these more ancient of peoples shared a much closer connection to the forces of Nature...with the capital "N"...representing the "giver of life," the provider of food, shelter, and warmth. One can find evidence today of these Prehistoric Cultures, dating to the Old Stone Age, approximately fifty thousand years ago. One finds some of the earliest examples of cave drawings, in Peking, in China.

That which most recognize as the beginnings of "modern man," the homo sapien, may have appeared on the Earth about forty thousand years ago, showing up first in Europe. What had suggested that this might be the demarcation line between lower forms of life and the human form was the partial preservation of the human and animal parts, suggesting that these articles may have been used in some sacramental way. The earliest sculpted form, found in these caves, were the "venus" figures, a crudely carved piece of stone, representational of the female form and fertility, as the giver of life. These forms generaliy exhibited an exaggeration of the hips and breasts, emphasizing the reproductive quality of Nature. It is believed that this hope for fertility then projected to fertility of the soil, in an effort at some magical control to ensure for the provision of food.

As these thoughts passed through my mind, there was a commotion at the far end of the camp. I noticed that Mog was dancing furiously about the edge of the fire, as if he were trying to convey something which might be relevant to the discussion. He was thrusting that pointed stick he carried at a nearby wall, on which were painted the generic shapes of what looked like animals. It appeared that this drama was being enacted to demonstrate his belief in the magic he expressed in preparing for the hunt, which was the event of greatest importance for his people.

He was jumping wildly up and down, beating his chest, and repeating something, which, to us, was unintelligible; but the repetitive nature of this chant seemed to have a power to it. At this point, Mog was again pointing at the drawing so crudely made on the wall, and this appeared to suggest a similar magical message, which celebrated the Man, as well.

These messages had been left on the walls of caves, and on the sides of cliffs; and they were that people's effort at transmitting knowledge between generations, and between peoples. It suggests that those humans, who had demonstrated the greatest power over the forces of Nature, perhaps in the form of their knowledge, or prowess, at hunting, became those figures upon whom the others looked for guidance and protection. It became incumbent upon these powerful figures to pass on their skills to the others. The paintings, you see, represented the skills which were being praised and taught. Lacking a greater awareness of the "laws of nature," Man attributed a great deal to the spirits he found in Nature, and which he could observe.

As there were so many different skills, and so many dangers to living, there were as many identifiable spirits acting on Man, each possessing its own sources of strength, and each offering its own wisdom for survival. At that time, when the first man walked the Earth, one would have believed that it would be the beasts which would have prevailed, being better suited to survival at birth. As a result, Man attributed some of the survival skills he had learned to these figures in Nature; and, from this, the resulting form of belief would have been *"animism"* a polytheistic form of belief, which praised the specific skills each figure thus represented. As yet unable to abstractly integrate these separate skills and powers into a unified force, polytheism allowed for separate and concrete forces.

Perhaps, it would be better to describe this as a *system of beliefs*, rather than a unified "religion." It was based on the more pragmatic concerns for day-to-day survival in a world which challenged them at every step.

It would appear that Man's ability to organize some integrated form of religion would demand that he first be capable of conceiving of some form of *sacred power*, some force which might transcend the physical world in which Man operated. This newly conceived force could do more than simply withstand the turmoil, which had been part of the daily struggle of each man. In its initial form, this force must have been perceived as a *duality*, with a masculine, and a feminine side.

The masculine force would represent the more aggressive side of Nature, and would exhibit a force used to *confront* life's challenges. On the feminine side, the force would be perceived as more *receptive*, representing the reproductive forces from which all of life emerges. Once this duality could be conceived, there could then have been the conception of a *struggle*, seen everywhere in Nature. And, at any point in which there is more than a single point of view, or force, one can conceive of two modes in which they might function; as *competing* forced vying for domination, or as *complementary* forces, which interact with the ultimate goal of simplifying the goal of survival.

I looked up, and noted that the gathering was getting restless. The skies were changing hue, and I noticed that something was floating out of the skies, and landing at the feet of those who were gathered. When I again looked up, I noticed Moses standing there, his staff raised, and he was offering thanks, declaring that we had been delivered *manna* from heaven. He looked down at where I sat, and said, "Beats the hell out of pizza delivery, don't it!"

I took a piece in hand, took a sniff, and felt the gentle texture. I gradually lifted it to my lips, and I took a small bite. I held it in my lips for a few seconds, and then I chewed it. 'Hmmmmm. Not bad. Kinda like whole grain, with honey and bran."

However, for each who partook, there was a different description of the taste, to each the flavor they most appreciated and was accustomed. It is obvious that manna is that of which each is most accustomed. I had to believe that the same might be true for the beverage, which was being collected from the nearby stream in pitchers. As I tasted it, I could taste the sweetness of wine, lingering on the palate.

This was a time for rest, and all drank their fill. There was some chatter, as the groups discussed the goings-on of the day thus far. The day was waning into night, and so we agreed to rest our minds for the night, and meet again the following morning.

I looked about me once more, noting the diversity of beliefs which were presented in the deities, but all were on friendly terms, despite their differences. It was very confusing, considering all the violence in the world, which had been enacted in the name of religion. But, if I had been able to understand all of this in the first place, I probably wouldn't be here now.

We just sat at the edge of the fire, watching the sparks as they ascended from the fire, and gradually dissipated in the air. We listened to the crackling of the wood, as the moisture was being drained from it by the heat of the flames. The night appeared to be calming, and the gathering gradually quieted. More began to drift off, as the fire warmed their faces. I remembered my Aunt Evelyn, looking down on the faces of my sleeping cousins, and saying, "Now, don't they look like dear little angels?" Knowing my cousins, *this* would have to be the only time of day this statement could be made.

But, with a look around this camp, I would be more than correct in making that same statement.

Chapter Four

I became conscious of the cool morning air, and was stirred by the "heavenly" aroma of freshly crisped bacon assailing my flaring nostrils. As I opened my eyes to greet the day, my eyes were momentarily blinded by the sunlight; so I rubbed away the cobwebs, which cloaked my vision, and looked at my side, seeking out the source of these wondrous smells. With a start, I realized that, there, beside me, with a great grin on his face, was the man who had been introduced as Moses. It took me a second or two, but it had finally occurred to me that, perhaps, my senses had been distorted somehow. So, I asked, "You?...Bacon!"

He looked in my direction, and smiled. "Don't worry, it's only *soy* products. But doesn't that *smell* really get to you? Boy! I *love* the smell of bacon frying in the pan!"

"But how do you get that aroma, if it's only a veggie?"

"Hey, it's no fun living with the deities if you aren't able to stretch the bounds of reality once in a while. Gods can do whatever they want...*if* their doctor lets them, of course." He puts his hand to his chin, pensively, and adds, "Maybe there may be some truth to what people have been saying about us on the streets".

"What's that?"

"They've been referring to those in "management" as *fat cats*"; and then he looked down at me. "Maybe we are, huh?"

"If you don't mind my saying, I think that, maybe, they were talking about management in terms of the *business* world."

Moses sat back, trying to display a look of being perplexed. "So, you don't think that we're management? Don't you think we get the big office, where all the *little people* come with all their problems, looking for *us* to make it all kosher? Sonny, if *this* isn't management, I don't know what is!"

"I guess you got a point there". The man had made sense; besides, who was I to put *him* in his place? Just consider; where does anyone turn when they are confronted with a dilemma of any sort? Even an *atheist* has to turn somewhere. Even if that's just turning to the man next to him, and so on down the line, somewhere, near the end of that line, *someone* will eventually turn his head upward, and offer up the questions.

I had to wonder how *they* dealt with the kind of stuff we humans turned to *them* for. "How do *you* guys deal with all that stress? I can see that you have urges for things, like bacon; does that mean you also have god-strength aspirin?"

Jehovah stroked his beard, looked down in my direction, and offered the observation, "Boychick, you certainly got the questions, don't you?" And he thought some more. "You know, sometimes the answers come easy to the deities...after all, our *job* is to come up with answers...But, a *good question...That's* sometimes a lot harder to come across. If you want to know the truth," and he stops here, and looks about him, at the others, "sometimes we just gotta hedge our bets a little. We offer answers which are designed to help keep their minds operating. They've always possessed the knowledge, whether they knew it or not. We just make them work a little harder, so they will find it themselves. You know how people are, they'd rather say that they did it themselves."

"Yeh!" shouted Buddha. "The Earth has been set up in the manner of a well-designed job site; everything you may need to complete any job is right there. It is up to each individual to make use of his god-given intelligence, combined with a modicum of creativity, and then, maybe, to lean on his buddies for a little help. Sometimes, it will take teamwork.

"A good question can be worth a thousand bad answers," offered Mohammed. "Even when you do all in your power to help them out, these humans take what they have been given, and then they distort it to such a degree that even *we* can no longer recognize it any more."

"Are you suggesting that the deities can be *fallible*?" There was a fixed stare on me from all around the camp. Had I overstepped by bounds? It was too late for me to offer up a prayer to save myself...and just *who* was it that I would pray to for help? The one's to whom I might have prayed were the same that I had just insulted here. Oy vay is mere!

The moment was tense, until the tension was broken by everyone's laughter, even Mog. Vishnu had leaned over to give me a friendly smack on the back, bent over, with tears in his eyes from the laughter.

"You guys always slay me, you know that?" Jehovah seemed to be speaking for the whole group. "You guys are always demanding so damned much from *us* that you never take the time, or even make the effort, at seeking the important answers for yourself".

"Personally, my favorite was George Burns, in that movie," observed Bodhisatva, with that slight twang of his Indian dialect. "I think that *George* offered a healthy, laid-back image of us. He told that guy...that John Denver guy...that all the tools were already there, right in front of him. For George, the only thing that he, as God, was asking of this character, was to let people know that He, God, was still around."

Jesus leaned forward, and rested a hand on my shoulder. "Sometimes, the answer can be *exquisitely* simple. But you humans can't just accept that, you got to read more into it, and make more of it than it is. They twist it, they turn it, and then they interpret it. Maybe...just *maybe*, they should just *listen* to it."

This spoken, I turned toward the assemblage, and said, "I shall do that very thing, and this moment. Besides, I haven't had a chance to have my breakfast, and, the way you guys eat, there may be nothing left if I don't start using my mouth for something more productive than talking."

"A smart boychick," grinned Moses.

And we all sat to break the fast.

As we ate, I had time to think over some of the things which had been presented, especially that which related to Mankind learning to make better use of what Nature and, therefore, God, had provided for him.

At this same time, I learned that the deities were both intelligent, and pragmatic; they used paper plates, so there was little, or no, clean-up. Being freed of cleaning up a mess, many took their morning constitutional around the grounds after breakfast. Many also performed various rites and ceremonies since, after all, many of the deities recognized by mortals, were themselves of mortal birth, and they still had to exercise their bodies.

At around mid-morning, all began to gather at the communal area. There was a great deal of chatter, with the one group, over here, discussing one thing, and another group, over there, discussing something else. However, down on the end of the camp, I could see that Mog was actively gesturing something, but I couldn't tell what. It was one of the tribal gods, related to Mog's heritage, and his beliefs, who tried to calm him. As he performed this process, he explained to me that *this* was one of the primary responsibilities of the earliest religious beliefs. Life and survival were centered in the family, or the clan, before it eventually expanded to engender *tribal* groups.

The rites and rituals had been designed around the family, or the clan, with the hopes of assuaging, or controlling, the gods, so that life might prosper and be safe. The lifestyle had always been harsh on people, and this made it the more important that communications, and connection, be constantly maintained, not only between the members of the family, but between Man and his deities. For most, the potential for eking out subsistence would be a full-time burden, even if everyone cooperated. Life had to be a pretty scary ordeal back then; the only thing of which there was any certainty, was that there was never any certainty. Man was at the mercy of Nature; and he would have to learn how to *read* Nature if he were going to be able to survive.

Once Man had learned the process for domesticating, or taming, certain of the animals in his environment, he was able to establish some small degree of certainty in his life. Up to this time, Man simply followed the seasons if he was to *find* food, in the form of vegetation, or herd animals. Man was the relatively passive recipient of Nature's presents. Of course, he had to work to get it, but his task was that of *gathering*, and not *producing*, food. He was at the mercy of Nature.

Once the animals had been domesticated, Man had a ready supply of protein from the meat, dairy products from the milk, warmth of clothing and shelter from the hides, and the beasts themselves to carry Man's burdens.

As he traveled between destinations, in search of his food, Man still required the capacity of carrying some food source along with him; and thus, he had to learn to *preserve and store* the foods. Unless the meats had been processed, by drying, smoking, or cooking, it could deteriorate quickly. He could eat only that which was at hand, and the rest would waste. Once he could process the meat, the dairy, and the hides, he found that he could keep the excess for those times when the pickings were slim.

Man learned to use the grasses and the barks of trees for protection. By beating them with sticks, or pressing them between flat stones, the materials could be toughened, flattened, and shaped into a woven cloth. By binding this cloth, they were able to create bags, to collect and carry the seeds, fruits and vegetables they would need. They could make cloth for garments, and for slings in which they could carry their young.

It is one of the wonders of that age than Mankind developed the ability to store and to cook, and, most likely, by accident. Who was the first to learn that, if the cloth bag were somehow coated with mud, or clay, and allowed to dry hard, it would not leak liquids, and it could withstand the temperature of a fire? This, then, would have been the first pot, or bowl. How would they have ever thought to place these vegetable fibers on the fire, in an effort at changing the texture and chemical composition of the foods, as a way of making them more digestible, even for the infants, so they might free the mothers from suckling, to perform other duties?

These technological advancements also did much to change the health of Mankind, freeing it of some of the ailments which had plagued Mankind due to contamination, or spoilage, or germs. Foodstuffs could be dried, processed, and stored in times of plenty, so they might be available when food was not available.

And the seed could be pounded and ground into flour, which, when mixed with water, could be baked into *bread*, which has to register as at least one of the greatest discoveries of Man, since bread is one of those *universal* foods, common around the Earth.

With the frailty of these resources in Nature, and in consideration of the toil which it took for man to eke out the most meager of lives, one is better able to understand the significance there would be in the protection of "territories," as defended by the clan, or the tribe, whether this be the traditional gathering circuit, or the tribal hunting lands. While the exact boundaries may never have been formally marked, it is certain that the boundaries were clearly passed on among generations as part of the inheritance of the group. If one studies many of the members of the animal kingdom, one will find territorial shows when another beast has entered what is protected by another.

Each such territory possesses its own level of productivity; and, in this way, the concept of "value" may have been added, leading to negotiations for the most productive lands as a guarantee of a future for one's clan. With productivity, was the ability of storing excesses, and to share the excesses with those in need. Each clan might be represented by some "totem," or spirit which inhabited the land, and which might enter the soul of the individual at birth. The land itself, *belonged to the gods*, whose totem, or spirit, was believed to reside in the earth. What the individual, or the clan, inherited was the *use of the land*, since no man could possess earth.

And the members of the clan defended their rights to these lands, and they gave thanks to the spirits of that land for its use in sustaining their lives. The female figures were those from which life could spring, in the manner in which the Earth gave up its food, and would nurture the animals which fed on it. The male figures were associated with qualities, such as strength and speed, which might represent the animals which they would hunt. All of those things which supported and fed the life of humans were given ritual forms and meanings. This included the elements of the weather, at whose mercy the early man existed, and which, to that early man, also appeared to have living, changing qualities.

The mind of man was still concrete in its ability to function cognitively, and its skills were focused on the immediate needs for survival. The deities, then, were also considered in the functional day-to-day survival of the species, and had not yet evolved the dealings with such concepts as virtue, or morality. No class structure existed, except that the strongest seemed to prosper from their developed abilities to sustain life, as did those in closest association to them. In general, survival was a struggle which was fairly equally shared by all. Each man was aware of the signs presented by Nature. There was, as yet, no need for a separate class of citizen with the ability of "reading" those signs for the others.

This was all very interesting, but I had to ask; "Why didn't Man leave well enough alone, then?"

A man of refinement, but of great years, arose from the group. "The economy began to change, and with it, Mankind was no longer tied to that immediate piece of land beneath his feet for survival. Man's source of economic well-being became more constant, as well as becoming more within the individual's control. How much he would prosper would depend on his natural endowments, and what he was willing to invest of himself; the seasons and climate alone did not run Man's life.

"He learned that there was greater stability of the land where the rivers and streams met, and formed river valleys, and fertile deltas. Man was able to tame the seed, the plants, the animals. He learned of irrigation, and of cultivation, and to rotate crops from season to season so as not to use up the nutrients in the soil.

"And with this growth, there was an ushering in of the rites and rituals, which served to connect these people together with a common thread. The stability of these people over time allowed for the evolution of "community". As elements within the community were able to develop certain skills, the rest of the community would rely on them to more effectively and efficiently perform these tasks, offering them a share of their own production, and, later, currency, for the product.

"There evolved a greater diversity of products, in service areas as well as the production of goods. There was a trade in the teaching of the skills themselves, being taught among generations, to be handed down, and passed on as a legacy. The responsibility of this process of passing on the knowledge became the domain of the elders, with the greater experience, while they, themselves, may no longer be capable of productive manufacture. Of even greater importance, these elders also possessed the greater skills in communicating that which they knew, so it would effect the next generation.

"As has already been noted, there is always the potential for informal communications to be distorted over time, and when transported distances, between peoples, and in differing languages. For this reason, Man established certain myths, and legends, which would withstand the test of time. Through these stories, he could establish cultural rules of behavior, which then suffered less chance of distortion or misinterpretation.

"Man was now responsible for more than his own subsistence, for the first time in history. With the reduction of the physical demands on the individual, and with the availability of products, the duration of human life had been extended in both years and usefulness. The elders who could no longer produce, could teach. The stories of the deities were designed to pass on a knowledge of skills important for survival, such as those which facilitated communication between the members of the group, establishing rites of behavior, including courting rituals, and establishing genetic breeding pools. Man was relatively ignorant of the processes of procreation, at least in a technical sense; but there was already awareness of genetic rules which were not to be transgressed. In this service, myths and lore had developed around the mating ritual, as a means of controlling the progeny.

"Until the development of written communications, all knowledge had been passed on by means of oral traditions. We are all aware of the distortions which are possible, whether intentional or not. Those traditions which proved to be the most productive, and the most protective of the integrity of the group as a whole, evolved into the rules of behavior. Being more specific in form now, there would be less chance of the distortions and misinterpretations which existed prior to this. To insure its transmission to the people, ceremony and myth grew up around this information.

"Man had always been in search of an identify of some sort, which identified him above all other creatures; and the development of his deity became a part of that identity, with each group selecting that image which would represent them, or their power. Along with this, there evolved a whole new class of individuals whose purpose would be to translate that knowledge of the deity into the common language of the people. There had already developed a division of labor within the economy; and now, this was extended to the religious practices of the clan.

"It had already been evidenced that, within the economic sector, those who could produce more, or better, products would gain in power or renown, developing wealth, and able to command tribute from their lesser tenants. This tribute might be in the form of sacrifice of some sort. By sacrifice, one might be talking of the donation of some portion of one's food, or clothing, or decorative items. When such tribute was paid by the wealthier citizen, the aim may have been to gain certain favors from the gods.

"One would not be surprised to learn of Man's attribution of human foibles to his deities. One need only remember the origins of the deities, such as Vishnu, Buddha, and Muhammed, who were born of Earthly seed. They had attained their lofty place only through the perfection of their strivings. Their service was to teach the rest of Mankind that they, too, could achieve such a place in the universe, this elevation above the mundane. However, each man being human, imbued him with human frailties and needs, which would have to be channeled and controlled. Rather than perceiving this humanness of origin as a weakness, Mankind was able to feel even closer with them, a greater sharing; and "humanness" would no longer be perceived as "weakness," but as one step along the path of living."

When it is put in those words, it really makes you take a look, and examine your own origins...spiritually, I mean. It makes this whole religion thing a bit more understandable. And it is easy to see that Mankind would develop a god which they could understand. For one thing, it facilitates communications, since, I guess, this says that we all speak the same language. It's not like I was going to be trying to communicate with some Martian, or something. The Twilight Zone, on TV, often had a field day with this concept. The innate fear of the "unknown".

Looking at it this way, one wouldn't be afraid of confronting his god. The image of a foreboding and all-powerful force has always gripped Man with fear; so, making one's god just "one of us" certainly makes it a friendlier belief system.

"Religion best serves Mankind as a stabilizing force, especially if they perceive themselves as being at the mercy of an unpredictable Nature. Mankind, and the land on which he relies, are inexorably linked as a single unit. Any spirit which can exist within Man, can easily be conceived of as existing in Nature. That is why people tend to anthropomorphize Nature; that is, giving it human characteristics, with which Mankind is already familiar."

"You mean, like...Earth to Earth, and dust to dust?"

"It has always been the belief of aboriginal man that *all* things in Nature hold a common life force; and thus, they deserve a measure of respect. By becoming one with that life force, one might develop the potential for power over one's fate. And, since the celestial bodies were equally mysterious to early man, the belief in them holding life is not uncommon.

"The skies changed, the seasons changed, the stars appeared to move in the heavens, the crops came and went, the herds migrated...and man was planted in the middle of all of this confusion. Those spirits, which eventually would dominate, can relate to some particular geographic location through which man had traveled. They can as easily relate to some necessity of a people, such as desert dwellers, and their dependency of the stages of the sun and moon. People of the tropics were more focused on the clouds, which brought with them differing rains. We may look to Hucheuteotl of the Aztecs, or Xiuhtecuhti in Mexico, or the gods of the Mayans and the Aztecs of Central and South America. Similar beliefs were found in the Andes of Peru, where Viracocha was the creator of life for the Inca.

'The gods became more abstract, and less directly tied to the land, as technology grew. New explanations flourished for the expansion of the Universe. Religions started to seek answers relevant to their expanding territory".

All I could think of was a saying that I had taped to the wall of my old office:

THE MORE WE KNOW WE KNOW,
THE MORE WE KNOW WE DON'T KNOW.

A lot to digest...And, speaking of digesting, I could see some food being delivered for our meal, and all were ready. Mog was already chewing on something, heaven only knows what; but the group around him decided to give him some room.

No sooner had I considered eating something, than I looked down, and there, before me, was a table, all set for the meal. It had occurred to me that it would be quite a job trying to satisfy the diverse tastes represented here. But, no sooner had I just *thought* this question to myself, than the venerable Lao Tzu, the founder of Taoism, pointed to my place at the table, and just said, "Know only that this is *the way*".

Chapter Five

There had been a great deal of hubbub at the far end of the gathering throughout the lunch break, predominantly among the Hindu deities. They had taken a marked interest in the morning's discussion, since they, among some of the other deities, descended from families of mortals. Among these deities were Shakti and Vishnu, who, together, next took the floor, and directed the discussion, derived from the cultural perspective with which they were most familiar.

"My peoples were derived from a wide diversity of cults, or sects, gathered from a wide geographical region, much as were the people of Judah. However, being of such a diverse group, perhaps they possessed a less well defined creed as the Jews, the Christians, or the Moslems. We shared some common identifying characteristics, which allowed us to function more like a unit. We are a simple people, gaining our livelihood from the earth; and, thus, had only the rudiments of a philosophy, nowhere as abstract as many others possessed. If the leaders were to have preached such an elevated philosophy, it would have placed them so distant from the people as to result in a feeling of abandonment. We, as a people, have been closely tied to the more menial levels of earth-dependence.

"The gods which these peoples envision must be men who were born of the Earth, and had experienced this life in its mortal sense, as did the people. It is only through the repeated reincarnations of the soul that these men have been able to learn the path which would allow them the peace of not "having" to return to this plane once more, to an existence which is defined by one's hard toil and diligence. The rewards which they could earn were sought through their never-ending labors, and through their many incarnations, until they could reach a level of being one with the ideal. This is the manner in which one becomes god-like. And it was something which was available to each and every man and woman, no matter their place in life. It is a similar philosophy to that of our friend from China, Lao Tzu, whose task was to teach "the way," or the "tao," a path which leads to the end of one's suffering as a mortal.

"These people, from the Middle East, are the same who created the earliest *living* body of religious literature in the world. They continue, to this day, to read from the Rig Veda, which is a collection of hymns, which appear to have developed in that period following the Aryan invasions into the lands which are now India, between the years 1500 and 1200 B.C."

I had always had some difficulty appreciating the complex and inflexible hierarchy of the religious hierarchies; and this made some sense to me, clarifying some of these concepts for me. These hierarchies had always seemed so *top-heavy* to me, with those who dominated in power stationed so far above the masses as to be almost inconceivable. If one is seeking a greater element of *democracy* in religion, then this could be at least one possibility. Still, I had to ask:

"If this was, indeed, such a loose confederation of diverse peoples, how could this be organized as a "religion"?"

It was Vishnu who next responded. "In each Hindu home, one finds the central focus on the "sacred fire," which is first kindled as part of the process of the marriage ceremony, and symbolizes the spark of life within the home. It is important that this fire never be extinguished, as it remains the focus of devotion within the home, the energy source in which flows the household spirit."

"Oh, I get it!" I interjected. "You mean that it serves the same purpose as the kitchen, in the traditional Jewish household?"

"This fire is the center of family culture. It's similar to many symbols found around the world. One may find an example of this "Eternal Flame" in Europe, Asia, Africa, South America. It symbolizes that link which exists between the individual and his ancestors. While, among the Hindu, the sacred fire links the individuals of the household with their ancestors, in America, and elsewhere, the eternal flame connects the citizens with those of their culture who may have given their lives for the cause of their people.

"Such a fire can provide a never-ending source of comfort for the people. It is there at their birth, it lights the path through their lives, and is the flame which may take them into their next life. In many cultures, as one's mortality wanes, one's mortal remains may be cremated in such a fire, and the ashen remains scattered back to the Earth, from whence it came."

"And this then initiates the process of the rebirth," added Shakti. "In this way, one's ancestors may be reborn in each of us, and thus, they take on a reverence and importance in our everyday life. For the Jewish, the ceremony of giving the child their Hebrew name is of this type of importance, for the child is always named for one of his relatives, that they may live on in this identity."

"It is through the efforts of our friends, Varuna and Mitra, that the physical universe finds order. The followers place markings on the body, recognizing aspects of the sect into which one may have been born. There are symbols which represent Vishnu, and Shiva. And then, each individual is given a very specific, and secret, *mantra*, or chant, with which to beckon his god. It is a powerful tool, but only so long as it remains unknown to any other. I believe that this, too, is common to many other cultures. The scriptures offer a secret name for their God, which may be silently chanted in some of their holiest prayers. The god of Egypt was known by several names, and each might be incanted for a specific purpose, or to a specific end."

"And there is yet another thing in common, to be found between Vishnu and Jesus of Nazareth, the God-figure of Christianity. The purpose for which Vishnu was given an earthly form was that he might save the world from destruction by the forces of evil. So, too, was Jesus. The Hindus believed that Vishnu was one of the persistently benevolent spirits, possibly a product of sun worship some period long ago. With the progress of time, the other earlier deities were gradually absorbed into the figure of Vishnu; who, as any Hindu, had returned in many lifetimes. Jesus, on the other hand, as part of his belief system, possessed but one visit to the Earth, for the purpose of making the people more aware of the presence of their God. So, Vishnu had repeated opportunities to purify the world, and, in each incarnation, perhaps, developing another following. Here, at this fire, I also see Rama, Krishna, and Buddha, who are said to all be incarnations of Krishna.

"And, while I am making comparisons, I would be remiss if I were to ignore the common elements which exist between the Hindu and the traditional Greek deities, such as between Vishnu and Achilles."

Again, an opportunity to make all aware of my own ignorance. "Achilles! Isn't that the guy they names the tendon after; you know, down the back of the leg?"

"Vishnu had lost his mortal life as a result of an accidental firing of an arrow, which found its mark in his only vulnerable place, being his heel. So, too, was the demise of Achilles."

The process of *living* is perceived of as a continuing cycle. Like Vishnu, himself, each individual is freed from this mortal body, only to be returned, in a new form. In the majority of cases, there is no real awareness of that former life, only a faint awareness and belief in a former existence. The task of each progressive incarnation is the seeking of a greater level of purification of the spirit. However, there have been stories of people who suddenly, and inexplicably, recover a memory of a former existence; and these experiences have been documented over the years.

"There is but one means of vacating this process of reincarnations, through the samsara, or the wheel of life. The process by which one frees one's spirit to reside in paradise is through making a choice *for total non-action*. It is deceptive, to be sure. It is a process which may fool many an individual. One must gain the awareness that passive action, such as the simple process of breathing, still may be defined as a form of "action". How does one measure "non-action" when one has only those tools which derive from action itself? Behavior is action. One can only measure the progress of non-action in the expressions of one's emotional investment, such as through "desire," and not action. It is the non-physical which binds one's soul to the ephemeral world."

It was at this point that Jesus spoke up. He appeared to be puzzled. "If I understand what you are suggesting, then there really may be little difference in our faiths. You define man's immortality through his many opportunities to return to the Earth, and numerous opportunities for improving himself, until he has earned the right to escape from this cycle of mortality. Am I Right?"

"That is so," offered Shakti.

"For those who would follow the tenets from which Christianity has evolved, one would know that one gains one's immortality through one's ancestry. If one perceives each such incarnation, of which you speak, as being a descendent of the original, then aren't we speaking the same thing? A Jew, a Christian, or a Moslem can lead a life of holiness; and he brings forth progeny, with the hopes of being actively remembered into the future. These memories, and the tales which are told of these lives, both serve to give that person a continuation of that life. In this same way, *any* of the deities gathered here can only find life if given that life by one's believers and followers. If the memory dies, the spirit may continue."

All I could think of was a line from the movie, <u>Oh, God</u>,! where John Denver turns to George Burns, and says, "Far-r-r-r-r Out!" In all of my studies, as an undergraduate and graduate student, in the fields of psychology and anthropology, I had never been able to put all of this together so neatly. I wondered, "Where could this go from here?"

I wouldn't have long to wait for the answer to this question, as I witnessed another rise from the group. I recognized the garb of India, but also wearing a cloth across the mouth and nose, and with bare feet. He identified himself as the leader of the Jains, and explained that the word Jain, in itself, stands for "The Unattached".

"As a part of our teachings, the Jains also teach that there exists a path to salvation for each soul. One enters this life free of any system of castes or classes, and possesses all the potential to attain that just and right path to Salvation. As part of this belief system, one neither conceives of, nor searches for, a universe which has any beginning or end; instead, it is a process of an infinite cosmic cycle. As has been taught us by the honorable Vishnu, there exists an ultimate reward simply for living the "right life." The reward is the escape from that wheel of life, and not having to return to one's mortal bonds.

"But, even more than this, Jainism is defined as the "path of non-violence". There is no eating of any animal life, including meat, fish, and eggs, but also all dairy, which supports life of the young of the species. The devout must go to great pains in an effort at bringing no harm to any life, even if it would be inadvertently. The holy walk barefoot, so as to sense the ground beneath them. They gently sweep the ground before them so as not to accidentally bring harm to anything. They wear the veil over their face to prevent the accidental inhalation of life. All creatures are cared for, and all manner of care is provided for the creatures of this world, no matter their potential for harming other life."

"Wow!" I thought to myself; that's pretty powerful. Looking at the world today, I could see a very different potential if all the world leaders were to live up to these beliefs. I had often thought of this world as something of a freak zoo; and, now learning this, I would want the keepers to be Jains. Then, I realized, that they could never have anything to do with such a place as a zoo. Their beliefs would not allow for them to capture any beast, and placing it in such an artificial environment. Man, I could see that I had a long way to go before I would ever have the strength, or the purity of heart, to successfully live a faith like that.

"Jainism also precludes the consideration of any *extremes*, or dichotomies. In such a belief system, there can be no such concept as something being "momentary," versus something being "eternal". The concept of *time* exists only as an illusion. All that exists remains in a constant state of flux, a continual change in both time and space. All things, which are born to this world, possess the qualities of *all* of the extremes. There is a power which the concept of "absolutes" holds on humans; by relinquishing this power, one lets in the power of "maybe," making *anything* possible. More of such beliefs among the peoples of the Earth might serve to relieve some of the frustrations of Man's existence, and alleviating some of the aggression which most people accept as a natural part of existence.

Furthermore, the concept of "salvation" is perceived as an *innate* capacity, born into each and every living thing. It is not the result of some form of intervention by some external force, acting on life, or of acts in the name of life. Instead, it is the result of an endless exertion of that individual toward his or her own attainment of "perfection". This being the case, there can be no *one* route to salvation; but, for each living thing, that path must be sought from within, using the potentials already available at birth."

Just then, there stood an impressive figure of a man, bearing a long black beard, a turban atop a mass of thick black hair. Others introduced this man as the Guru Nanak, celebrated for his teachings by the Sikhs, also an Indian people, descended from the Punjab.

"I share many of these beliefs, which have thus far been presented, from both the Moslem and the Hindu. I cast out any belief in idolatry, and I practice the inward, and silent, devotions of the ascetics. My belief is in God as a *unity*; but He is *unknowable* through the senses, only to be known through the heart. And, in that way, I am also in agreement with the Jewish faith.

"However, I also perceive mortality as a form of "bondage" to the human condition. It is "of-the-world"; and, thus, it cannot be trusted. Much of what is presented to the senses on this Earth cannot be trusted, as it may all be deceptive, as was suggested by our friend, Aristotle. That which exists in this world may be no more than an imperfect reflection of some ideal, which can only exist in its perfect state in one's conceptions, or on another plane. For this reason, it is always recommended that no man become overly attached to the things of *this* life. This could possibly blind him as to his true earthly role, and it could prevent him from attaining his eventual path to salvation. It is for this reason that I believe that all things, which may cloud the mind, must be banned."

At his side, another figure interjected, "The Buddha-Sasana are another group, which reside both in India and into China". Vishnu reached over, and offered this man a supportive pat on the shoulder, introducing him as Siddhattha.

"For these people, the Buddha is representative of "the way of life," and, in its direct translation, it means "the discipline of the Awakened One". For those amongst us who have been raised to perceive of their gods and spiritual leaders as being above humanity, one must keep in mind that many of these spiritual leaders gathered here were of mortal birth, as was I. I was born about the Sixth Century, B.C. that is, in the north of India. I was born to a poor family, the Gotama. My given personal name was Siddhattha. The beliefs which I follow, however, can be dated back nearly 120,000 years.

"What I share in common with the others of Indian heritage is the belief that all in life deals with *this* place in the world, and with *this* time in history. My ambitions, however, have always been to seek a state of awakening, and an awareness of another realm of being beyond this. I recorded my beliefs, and my stories, in the language of the Pali, which comes from the north of India, and is one of the oldest languages of this world.

"Like the others, also, my search has been for an answer to Man's eternal suffering, at the hands of the cruelties of his life, and of existence itself. I have always believed that one's ultimate reward would be to be returned to the soil, from whence one rose. Buddhism, at least as *I* preached it, was an ascetic form of life, one involving strict discipline, seeking a release from the futility of life on this Earth, and offering to each the liberation from this weariness.

"In order to search out this path, in this particular manner, I chose to live my life on the Earth as a "shamana," a holy person. But, even this failed to get me closer to my goal. What I was truly seeking transcended existence itself; I was seeking an eternal realm of being, which may only be known in Nirvana, a place which lays beyond this world. Before this can be sought, however, it becomes each person's mission on this Earth to first conquer the *evils*, which are ever-present in this life.

"But, even once one has had the grace of attaining Nirvana, the choices remain. While the journey is exhausting, the easy path would be to choose to remain in Nirvana, enjoying those well-earned rewards for the life which had been positively spent.

"It was *my* choice to leave that state of grace, and to return to the mundane world, in an effort at helping those who have also sought their own personal "awakening," to help them find the path. That is why I am also known by the name Bodhisatva, which stands for "He who returns from the edge of Nirvana."

"There are so many beliefs being represented here," I said. "What is it that one must do in order to seek this "awakening," of which you speak? Is it a matter of one's birth, or one's achievements, or...*what!*"

"These beliefs are freely preached to *all* the people. There is no demand for membership of any kind, or for any special qualifications; it is truly egalitarian in this way. It demands no special sacrifices, no fees, and it represents no caste, or class system. I understand that there are those belief systems which have been taught only to those who can speak, or read, some special dialect, or language, such as a language familiar to aristocrats alone. The instructions of the Buddha use the simplest and most familiar forms, such as the parables, similes, and anecdotes, the very type of thing which has always been common to these people in communications within the family system."

"Fascinating! You mean that I've actually found a system in which *everyone* can be *absolutely* equal!" This is something that many systems had forever preached, but very few had qualified at.

"Oh! Perchance I may be misleading you here...there *does* exist a hierarchy. However, it is based purely on each individual's *efforts*, and it does not represent wealth, or aristocratic bearing. It is based solely on levels of "respect". Within the wheels of life, the cycles of leaving and returning to this life, the individual possesses repeated opportunities for attaining his or her own goals, whatever they may be; and, with each such gain, there is an ascension on the wheel. It is thus based on such factors as mortality, meditation, and wisdom, which, of course, are a great source of wealth...but qualities which cannot be purchased with Earthly moneys.

"Buddhism translates the word "wisdom" as meaning "the truths of life". By this wisdom, mortality is perceived as one of the ills of this existence, as is its impermanence. Nothing remains unchanged and immutable. All things which are available to the senses are in a constant state of flux, which is as true of the soul within each man. It is the mission of each man to fight for that "eternal soul," in which he believes. Each man must face those elements which serve as blocks to his salvation, which exist in a physical form, in sensations, in perceptions, in volition, and in consciousness.

There is *no* enduring *mortal* soul. If there were, its existence could serve only to define the individual in the here-and-now, which would thus represent self-interest, rather than the seeking after the common good of Mankind. My perception is a wider conception of life; one which transcends the *I*, the *me*, and the *mine*. In this way, it reflects the thinking of Twentieth Century thinkers, such as Abraham Maslow, the psychologist, who conceived of a *hierarchy of needs*, which he symbolized in a pyramid. At the base of this pyramid, the widest and most supportive segment of the structure, were those necessities for the survival of the mortal body, such as sustenance, shelter, and clothing. At the peak of this pyramid, and seekable only once the earthly desires have been adequately met and stabilized, were the "self-less" needs, which were considered to be desire-free."

Hmmmmm. How would a person go about getting such a cleansing, I wondered. "What does one have to do to become a priest in this religion?"

"It is the responsibility and the duty of every believer to participate, and to become a monk, casting off the earthly desires in search of a cleansing of the spirit. Each believer freely offers a share of his earthly sustenance in order to feed and clothe these monks. It is in no way suggested that the monk is anything but a common man; indeed, it is a sign of his average existence, a simple existence which we will share. The cleansing is found through the ascetic life, which this sharing is enabling.

"However, this is a temporary mission, for each man is expected to return to the lay life, which is required so that he may advance the cause of his family, his group, and Mankind in general. The temple is a very basic place, at which life is simple, with even simpler goals. It involves very little in the way of competition; and that, in itself, may release a great deal of man's energy for seeking that peace *within* him."

I liked that; it made a lot of sense to me. All I had to compare this with was the life I had, to now, led; and *that* now seemed so chaotic in comparison with what was being presented here. In Western Civilization, life seems to be a constant battle to "get ahead," whether it be a battle for grades in school, on the sports field, or fighting for status and fortune on the job. And then, even if one is lucky enough to "make it," one only has to worry about the next guy, who, like oneself, has set his eye on *you* as his next goal.

Grumbling could be heard among the gathering, with many wanting to be heard. Each had his own views on life, and each, of course, deserved to be heard. I had found no natural order of leadership in this group; but, gradually, some natural order to things was slowly disclosing itself. Examining the proceedings thus far, I could see that it had been the ancients who had first offered their wisdom, starting with our friends from prehistory. From there, the discussion seems to have followed an evolutionary path. If this were true, from my studies in anthropology, I would suspect that the Orientals might be the next to share.

And, as these thoughts entered my head, I could see Confusius enter the fray.

"Exactly who is the oldest of the cultures, this is an issue for some debate, I'm sure. However, of this one thing I can be certain; the philosophies of the Chinese peoples represent the largest population, in both area, and in the diversity of peoples involved. It is also our reputation that we are among the most successful in remaining isolated from the prying eyes of the outside world. We have not served as missionaries, nor have we tried to force our beliefs on the rest of the world. In its basic teachings, the oriental philosophies have focused on the ancestral family.

"Again, while there may be debate as to the oldest recognized culture, there can be no argument that the Chinese possess the longest history of developing administrative and organizational skills. What was passed on from generation to generation was less of a religious belief, as it was a *tradition*, and its teachings.

"I am humbled in professing to the origins of this path; I, Confusius. There was never an institutionalization, or cultism. The social aspects of Confusionism have been governed by a practice of "divination," practiced through the reading of the ancient artifacts; thus, gaining knowledge from the ancestors. This practice maintains the strength of the family, by maintaining the connection between the generations. One's ancestors have always been inseparable from one's present-day functioning.

"As is the case with many of the more so-called "primitive" cultures, ours has a history of practicing "animism," which also included the fertility cults. However, with the rise of the

Shang Dynasty, in 1207 B.C., and then extending into the Chou Dynasty, religious beliefs gradually evolved into prayer to our ancestors, to help us in this day of toil. In this system, it was Shang-Ti who became known as the "Supreme Ancestor," or the T'ien. Within this figure was represented all of the heavens and the Earth, and held the totality of all which ever was, and that which continues to be. In its economic form, it could be called a feudal state, or one in which the king also served as the priest for the people, the messenger between Man and the ancestors. In its earliest stages, these priest-kings were also the war-lords, and the ceremonies made to the ancestors may have included the human sacrifice of captives, who had been defeated in battle.

"I existed, in my mortal form, from 579 to 551 B.C., and I made much use of the ancient writings, my goal being to restore the values and practices of the Golden Age of Chou. However, in my effort at making this process more palatable for the people, I also offered my more contemporary interpretations of these writings, which served to alter this faith from a system which was based on such things as luck and fate, to a belief in the moral and ethical path, of right and wrong.

"In my life on this Earth, I worked as a simple itinerant trader, moving from place to place, bartering my wares, and introducing items from one area to another. But, this also offered me the opportunity of traveling widely, and gathering a great diversity of knowledge which could not be known to any one area alone. I observed the different peoples, and I could see what may have been lacking in their lives, and made note of this. In my mortal form, in truth, I believed that I possessed no great influence on the thinking and beliefs of my people; but, after my death, there were those who had listened to my discussions, and they had written them down in a form known as "the analects".

"According to my observations, my teachings described the ideal path which one might take through this life, which was called "the way of the true gentleman," a system of personal morality and ethical conduct. This path was innately born in every man; it was but for him to seek and strengthen it through his interactions with others on this Earth. Confusionism is a focus on the individual's service to Man, and not a service to the spirits. Through this process, each learns from one's ancestors, who represent the real spirits in each of our lives. As a belief, it focuses on a belief in justice to the common man, which is known as Min, rather than being a form of praise only to the aristocracy, known as the Jon. And, I believe, we have much in common with our friends Martin Luther and John Calvin, especially clearly stated in the words of one of the followers of Confusius, known as Mensius. He stated that "a constant mind without a constant livelihood is impossible"; which, to me, suggests that we must each actively live our beliefs, through our work in this world, and our work for the good of our fellow man.

"In this endeavor, there exists an innate good in man, which we define as the Hsing, or human nature; and this must be properly nurtured. A second force which acts on life is the Ming, or fate, which is perceived as the working of heaven's hand on our life. Once again, there are commonalities with other beliefs. In this case, I accede to our friend, Aristotle, who also suggested that moral order and perfection are simply creations of the mind, and thus, are the center of the universe. Our philosophies are defined as "activism," and are thus seen as worldly."

"Much of the life, which is practiced by those in the Orient, is, at its very base, more of a "philosophy" of life, a study of the principles which underlie the *conduct* of man more than perceived as a religion, at least in its formal sense." These words were offered by the man identified as Lao Tzu.

"For myself, the philosophy became known as the Tao, or *The Way*. I believe that this philosophy is more comfortable for those who reside in the countryside than it was to accept the teachings of Confusius, whose ideas predominated in areas of denser population, and thus, a more sophisticated system. In the countryside, the people appear to be more *contemplative*, and focus more on taking the time to think an idea through, rather than simply turning to action. They seem to have the ability to envision the other-worldly, and are more capable of seeking a state of *peace*, which exists within each individual. There is more of the *mystical* in the beliefs of those from the countryside.

"I have written that the Tao is *one*, into which all things may blend, and therein they may remain. The Tao is a spontaneous, and a continuous, process, which continues through *this* life, and the *next*. Any human institution, developed for the purpose of governing human thought, could do nothing but interfere with the normal flow of the Tao. The flow of existence is *continuous*, and so, that which humans may conceive of as *death*, may only be one of the many stages of living. One is ever in a process of changing form, through varying stages of the same process. I understand that there is a Western writer who speaks of similar things, expressed in the modern era; someone named Elizabeth Kubler-Ross, who has written a book, <u>On Death, And Dying</u>. In one of her later books, she comes to describe the process of dying as being the final stage of "living"...and yet, it remains a stage of *life*.

"There can be no difference between what we perceive as life, and what we perceive as death; they are but varying forms of the same thing, which is the *spirit of man*. Within this philosophy, there is also the conception of a unity of "right" and "wrong". If one should be true to the philosophy of Taoism, in its most conservative form, one would avoid the concept of death itself."

Well, I just couldn't let a straight-line like that go by. There's that smart-ass in me that just can't leave well-enough alone. So, in honor of that great philosopher, Rodney Dangerfield, I had to say, "Yeah, I guess that I can understand the philosophy, all right; but there's just one problem that I find with most of these Oriental religions I've studied."

In unison, Buddha, Confusius, and Lao Tze asked, "And what would that be?"

"Well...An hour after praying, I just feel hungry again!"

"Booooooooooooooooooooo" was the unified response from the assemblage.

'That's O.K. I deserved that one."

"Yes, you did."

"But, you know, children today tend to be open to all kinds of new thoughts; but I guess one could say that they can be pretty gullible, as well. It's not like days past, when the greatest thing was to sit with a good book, and trying to create a magical world in your mind to match that of which you read. Today, much of what kids are presented is not meant to train them for deep thinking. Their attention span tends to extend about as long as the average music video, and that's about it.

"But, they were affected by such things as that TV miniseries, Shogun. Not only did it convey a sense of life at that time, but it presented excitement and danger, which raise the pulse of most kids. After that program, you could find kids walking around, and playing with their own version of the samu-rai sword, trying to imitate the Japanese warrior.

"The question which this brings to my mind relates to a philosophy which talks of meditation, but displays such violence. How do these elements find balance on the islands of Japan?"

A man rose. "I am known to the Ainu people as Kami, and I am a lord of the cosmos. My people are an ancient island people, who lived a life of great sacrifice and hardship. In return for their suffering, they often demanded blood sacrifice, and declared that their own recorded era of history be defined as the "Age of Kami". If one examines its origins, one finds that the original shaman of the people was female, which made it easier to conceptualize as an "Earth-Mother," and possibly an extension of what Mog, down there, would have represented in his Venus-figure.

"Out of this philosophical development evolved "The Way of Kami," which later became popularized as *Shinto*. The aim of this Shinto lifestyle was to *directly* experience the divinity, through each and every one of the mysteries that life on Earth can offer. While many of the other philosophies, such as Confusionism, had become intellectualized, through the use of intricate words, concepts, and rites, Shinto refused to focus on the cognitive alone, and emphasized an appreciation of the world of the spirit. Thus, Shinto is not a cognitive philosophy, because the Kami, itself, is *ethereal* by nature, and can only be truly known, or experienced, *intuitively*.

"Is this not similar to the God of the Jews? Is he not also a spirit of the heart, more than of the brain?"

"How come I've never seen a Shinto temple?"

"That is because Shinto is a philosophy which remains simple, for the common man. Its focus is on the simple daily functioning of the average person in this world. The rites of the Shinto are simple indeed, performed in small shrines, which are most often found in the family home, or alongside a commonly traveled path. It is most commonly practiced in the home, amongst the extended family unit.

"The Shinto seek after four basic themes, or steps, to its practice. The first step represents the *cleansing* process, by which the Earthly waste may be removed. In the second step, the Harai, one performs the act of purification. The third step is called the Shinsen, which is a formal act of "offering" to the spirits. And the final step is the Naori, a form of symbolic feast, which is carried out in honor of Kami."

As this explanation of the Shinto is explained, I had to sit back in my seat, just in an effort at trying to digest what had been presented. Though we may have actually examined hundreds of thousands of years of Man's existence on this Earth with our discussion, one can certainly find some common threads running throughout these civilizations. Too often, we seek out and find only differences, which serves only to fuel hostilities. Each of these philosophies seems to be initiated as a down-to-earth means of understanding the complexities of the world around us. Maybe this is because Mankind has been so dependent on the seemingly whimsical offerings of the Earth toward Mankind's survival here.

The mother-figure is another one of those features which are apparently common to many peoples, something of a universal concept, first found in the Venus-figures as far back as the Stone Age, as well as being represented by the Madonna and Child, an icon of modern Christianity. The association made from this is neatly drawn, and is very direct. According to this conception, which is one of simplicity, and common to all forms of life, life is formed within the *womb* of the Earth, and is pushed out into the surface world, in the form of food-stuffs, as well as animal life.

If one examines this concept closely, one will note that the caveman was no idiot; he was aware that where there is life, there had to exist the two entities, which made that life possible. For them, the division of labor was clear; the female represented *fertility*, and the sensitivity of the Earth, while the male represented the more *aggressive* and active figure, whose job it would be to hunt for the food, and to defend the family unit. It is possible that one might find this same duality in the Asian principles of the Yin and Yang, in the masculine against the feminine, in the dark against the light, and the strong against the sensitive.

While most civilizations present themselves as masculine, or male dominated, the image of the gods has never really been *that* clear. In most known cultures, the totality of the spirits actually existed in the *one*, in a form of unity. While most of the icons, which represented these gods, appeared to be masculine in gender, in actuality, they tended to possess a duality of male and female. Should one seek evidence of this, one need only look at some of the art of India, which, sometimes, can make the distinguishing of sexual identity difficult...and, I think, it was meant to be so. In the rendering of "The Last Supper," the image of St. John is almost universally feminine in nature. This is not to say that one is rendering weakness into a masculine character; on the contrary, it may very well be portraying one of the strengths of this character. What may be shown is more than the raw strength of the masculine character, but the perseverance, and the passive strength, of the female traits...

Ah, but I ramble. These thoughts are but my own; so, I beg forgiveness. The hour has been getting late, and we had not paid heed to it. Mealtime is approaching, and it is time for rest.

Looking to the far end of the gathering, one could tell that Mog was again becoming impatient, and those around him were certain to give him his space.

The gathering sat back, and all partook of a pleasant meal. The talk went well into the night, covering all the areas of the day's activities. Some of the participants were determined to defend their own particular bias, as if this were some form of honor; and these were the ones that demanded that there could be no possible diversion from some *absolute* truth, which they held, and which, of course, *only they* happened to know. However, most of those congregated here were tending more toward some common ground, where more ideas were shared than argued.

All in all, this was turning out to be a very enlightening experience.

Yet, I remained encumbered with the question of just *why* all of this had taken place. In the presence of some of the materials thus far collected, it was becoming easier to "go with the flow," than to attempt combat with each new idea as it was presented.

All of this brings to mind something which occurred to me years ago, when I was in graduate school, and dealing with the topic of ideologies. We were presented a philosophical problem, which involved a man, who was envisioned approaching a raging river, and seeking to reach a particular point on the far shore. Seeing his target clearly, he jumped into the river, and flailed madly in an attempt at fighting the current, and reaching that point on the other shore. In the end, of course, he exhausted himself and was simply carried away with the current, and only able to pull his exhausted body to shore at a point much further downstream. After an extensive period of recuperation, he drew himself to his feet, and walked the long distance to his original goal site.

A second man approached the river's edge, with the same goal in mind. However, upon observing the current, it was his decision to travel back upstream a short distance by foot, and there, he entered the water. Instead of fighting the current, this man was able to use the current to carry him downstream, and he aimed himself on a diagonal course. He emerged at his target site with ease, and was able to immediately go about his chores without any delay, or any excessive expenditure of energy.

And, what does that have to do with the present situation, you ask?

Well, I guess that I shall give myself to the current, and see where it shall take me.

And so, the night came upon us; and I gave in to sleep.

Chapter Six

I wasn't sure exactly what time it was when everyone was stirred from his repose by a commotion, down at the far end of the gathering. Sure enough, one could barely make out the form of Mog, dashing about from place to place, wielding that big club of his. He was at it again, beating the ground with that thing that he had torn from a nearby tree. Evidently, he was trying to catch some poor critter, which suggested to the rest of us that it must be getting time for some breakfast. Finally, one of the people nearest to him grabbed his arm, and tried to offer him some of the food, which had been prepared for the gathering. At first, he just stared at it, this burnt piece of flesh, which sat on a pewter plate. He sniffed at it for a minute, but looked quizzically at the others. Some of them were gesturing with their hands, pointing toward their mouths, and trying to convey to him that this was indeed something to *eat*.

Tentatively, Mog put a small bit of this substance into his mouth, and he let it just sit there for awhile, uncertain of how to process it. Then, he chewed a few times, and swallowed hesitantly, waiting for a reaction. Once he had swallowed, a big smile spread across his hairy face, and he stuffed the rest of the food into his mouth. He jumped around, and grunted with satisfaction, gesturing for more. Dining manners were obviously not Mog's strong suit; and, watching his gusto seemed to have put off many of those around him. While his appetite was voracious, many of the others appeared satisfied with whatever they had managed to eat before Mog had eaten his. Someone commented; "Well, you've got to admit, this certainly goes a long way to focusing one on one's own table manners, doesn't it?"

The mood was much more congenial this morning, with fewer arguments breaking out during the meal. One of the more refined of the deities rose; "It would seem that the more we learn about each other, the less bickering that develops. The more we know, the less we find in variance amongst our beliefs. And, it certainly seems to be advantageous for our digestion, this lessening of tension among us."

Our discussion had, to this point, offered a view of early man, and some of the more ancient systems of belief, expressing the manner in which Man offered up prayer to the spirits in whom he believed, and in their manner of daily functioning in the real world. It appeared that what we accept and define as "modern civilization" started around the year 3000 B.C., in and around the Fertile Crescent, in the area later known as Mesopotamia, or the Tigris-Euphrates Valley.

"Religion and philosophy grew up together, the one indistinguishable from the other. The same may be said to be true of what has become known as "science," too. It was in the Eighteenth Century that one started to see a distinction of study into the "human sciences," initially presented under the heading of philosophy in most European universities. That which became the "sciences" were predominantly defined by the experimental method, an attempt at making all observations, and, thus, the conclusions made from them, as objective as possible. By objective, I mean that any individual who observes the data would most likely come to the same conclusions. Up to this time in history, knowledge was "subjective," a personal interpretation of the evidence presented to the senses. As I remember it, it was not until the establishment of the first physiological psychology laboratory, by Wilhelm Wundt, at the University of Leipzig, in 1789, that psychology was finally granted an identity apart from philosophy."

This discussion fell to those empowered in the early development of European studies. "Many of the early studies delved into the arena of the creation of the universe, and Man, as this was perceived as remaining one of the few stable areas of belief since the cosmic origins of the Earth. Both religion and science were in search of the cosmic meanings of life, and seeking out the unchanging order of things in the universe. These studies focused on *belief*, rather than on *logic*. Scientific study was later to be guided by the "laws of nature," those invisible and stable tenets of life itself; however, man was yet unaware of these. The general rule, which prevailed, was that Man simply accept the natural phenomena as they were presented in life, and not to question it. Science was thus as dogmatic as was religion. Thus, one finds that technology developed in the absence of true science until some later time.

"The believed origins of Mankind rested in the soil, the earth which rested under foot, and from the mud which stood at the water's edge. Religion, then, was also firmly evolved from the soil. The mysteries of life, and the perils of living, could only be perceived as being marginally within the control, or even the understanding, of Man. To the average man, these phenomena were controlled by the *unknown*, and, perhaps, the *unknowable*. As such, the forces of nature appeared to be whimsical.

"Thereafter, there developed the "urban revolution," wherein the population began to congregate at certain focal, and common, areas. People were now joined to each other by more than just the soil, and this forced them to rethink their existence, and their beliefs. It was in this manner that the Earthgods started to fade from importance as society became less dependent on the soil for its survival."

Just then, I noticed someone in a costume of some sort, with a headdress, moving in the morning air. "Who's that?"

"That's Isis. Pay careful attention, my friend, for it may have been on the basis of her civilization that many of the Middle Eastern philosophies later evolved." So, I shut up, and listened.

"Before there were civilizations along the Eastern Mediterranean, there was Egypt, whose life poured forth from the giving hand of the Nile. The bounty which resulted from the overflowing of her banks each year gave birth to the crops, on which the people survived. By this dependence on such a whimsical source of life, there evolved a polytheistic form of religious belief, offering its thanks to those powers which brought forth life, each in its season.

"In their awe of the unknown, and the unpredictable, the forces of Nature themselves were deified, each given its place in the story of creation, and in the survival of the people. These were forces over which the people felt they had no control, and they beseeched these forces for the bounty which they could provide.

"Mankind was aware only of its own dynamics, and they would project this onto the gods that they created. Among these characteristics was that of jealousy, now seen as a force between the gods. The most powerful of these gods was myself, Isis, the goddess of fertility, the giver of life. The other gods, in their jealousy, captured me, and separated me into seven parts, scattering each part to another region of the known world of the time, and burying it. In time, each of these parts of the whole had gained the power of a "totem," and each possessed an identity of its own. We have found similar phenomena among modern man. Each separate part was identified as a god in itself, and each so labeled, with a design for its worship established. However, in the end, all of the parts were only a part of "The One"."

"Aye! And it is from this seed that the Celtic faith of the Druids did grow," shouted a voice from the crowd. "It is well accepted among the scholars that this agrarian culture of the British Isles had its birthplace in Egypt, finding its way north by the great ocean journeys."

At this moment, I noticed Jesus leaning in my direction; and so, I turned my ear to him. With the hint of a smirk on his face, he whispered, "That's funny; he doesn't look Druish! Ha-ha-ha!" There was no other reaction to the remark, except a comment from someone in the rear; "Maybe you'd better just stick with the work of salvation, huh, J.C.?"

"We, the Druids, share many beliefs which had been absorbed into the culture as a result of our close ties to the soil, and to Nature. Our dependence on the soil led us to offer praise, and even human sacrifice, to those gods which sustained us through good times and bad. Our rites celebrated the harvest, focusing, as it did, on the Sun and the Moon, in their varying phases. We celebrated the time of the planting, and the time of the harvest. Our culture followed the pace which was set by the equinox, as the Sun made its crossing of the Equator.

"We sought to record this journey of the celestial bodies, and we did so at a site which was known as Stonehenge, outside of the town of Wroxton, in England. Though many of the stone we placed there have since fallen, and their order confused, I believe that this site continues to tell a story of the heavens, to those who know how to read it."

As the Druid was completing his tale, there arose a large figure, and on his neck he wore Olympic medals.....No, I mean *real* Olympic medals!...from Mount Olympus, itself. Many of those near him, who were dressed in similar regalia, bowed as he presented himself.

"In carrying out my responsibilities as the leader of the gods on Mount Olympus, I, Zeus, have observed the gradual spread of civilization throughout the Mediterranean region. The seeds of Homeric thought were planted, and, while strong in philosophy, that culture had not yet developed any of the formal institutional dressing, which one would expect to go with it. It appeared to be absent of creeds, and it spread in the absence of what would be called true articles of faith.

"I have learned that many are the men, who teach the words of their beliefs, identified as "men of god"; but, in truth, those who taught among the Greeks were perceived more as public officials, rather than as interpreters of the words of the gods.

"The gods, themselves, were *reified*; that is, they were given human form and identity, which the common man could accept and understand, helping him to function effectively in day-to-day living. For the common man, it was an easier task to conceive of a benevolent force, which carried a recognizable form, rather than being asked to believe blindly in some unseen, and imperceptible, consciousness. Though the acts of the gods may have seemed whimsical at times, it would be easier to attach human form to such a phenomenon. I believe that this practice, of giving human attributes and traits to the mystical forces in Nature, has become known as *anthropomorphism*, is it not?

"By this same process, it was Man's attempt at perceiving a world in which he lived as being less filled with terrors, and more familiar to his needs. In this same way, then, Man sought to give definition to some of the less comprehensible experiences which existed in his inner psychological world, which had, till then, remained mystical and fearful. This process enabled Man to more objectively examine the phenomenon of the "Self," and perceiving it as something which might exist apart from that inner world. To explain this, let me offer an analogy.

"Let us imagine that there is a man, who has ventured too far from the shore of a lake, and is in danger of drowning. As he struggles for each breath, his entire focus is on his own survival, and he is unable to appreciate the natural beauty of the surroundings. However, by setting a distance from his plight, such as having him stand on the shore, a clearer perspective of the scene might be gained. With each such step from the shore, one continues to gain perspective, such as the view of the lake within the setting of the woods, and gaining a better grasp of all the realities which impinge on this scene.

"Man is capable of taking a shapeless terror, and molding it into a visibly beautiful form, which he can then appreciate. It is in this manner, also, that Man projects himself into his perception of the gods. This process also enables Man to *externalize* his relations to the *self*, to his *society*, and to *Nature*. Man could feel comfort in approaching another human form, and in interpreting that individual's behavior; and, in this way, the gods became more approachable.

"However, in the process of this happening, the church and the state became inseparable, wherein the gods were identified as heroes of the state, at least as much as the heroes of man could become gods. Each decision which was to be taken by the state, in the name of the people, would be passed before the gods, at the temples, which also represented the state's public buildings.

"There would be no potential for a "unity of divine law" developing so long as there were so many differing gods, each representing certain identifiable rights. It became difficult for the readers of the law to clearly identify "right" from "wrong," as each act could be interpreted differently by each different god.

"It was actually Plato, I believe, who attempted to transform theological thought. And it was Aeschyles who took the image of Zeus, as he had been presented by Homer, and attempted to portray him as a unifying force among the gods. This, of course, was not such a new idea; it had already been achieved among the Jews, as represented in their conception of Jehovah, as the one and only God.

"The Earth-bound symbols of religion, which had existed up to this time, were very appealing to the *imagination* of Man; but they lacked the value of real learning, and taught few lessons on life and living. However, what the philosophy of the Greeks *did* seek was to appeal to the *intellect*, by extending this from an "image" to an "ideal". Plato had stated that "things," that is, entities which could take on form, were only a fleeting representation of some ideal reality. These "representations" were *always* subject to change; the "ultimate reality," however, was unchangeable.

"Knowledge is pure; that which can be observed with the senses can only be an imperfect reflection of that ideal reality."

"And thus, we are drawn to the evolution of Judaism, the next step in this chain," resounded a voice behind me. As I turned my head, I was staring directly into the eyes of Moses, certainly an imposing form, with flowing gray hair, and flowing beard of similar hue.

"If we are going to keep this historically accurate, one might have presented the plight of the Jews first; but I am well aware of the jockeying for position which is occurring. Of course, I'm not suggesting that there truly exists an actual *hierarchy*. As a matter of fact, I believe that *that* might be the one outstanding point which has developed out of this whole discussion."

His point being made, Moses shifted slightly, and joined Jehovah and Jesus at the fire's edge. They spoke amongst themselves for a bit. But my own ignorance of religious history was even worse than my awareness of the diversity of beliefs which had existed through the ages; so, I decided to ask, "When, exactly, would you place the origins of Judaism?"

The three looked silently at each other, and then Moses, the orator among them, was selected as their spokesman.

"The real history of the Jews, as a *people*, can be traced back as far as three thousand years ago. But, even this is no simple task, the tracing of Judaism as a united belief. To simplify matters, many associate the rise of Judaism with the exodus from Egypt. But, that is only an association which may be made with the Land of Judah, and the founding of the first Jewish state in the Middle East."

Jehovah leaned forward, thoughtfully stroking his chin. "I am aware of many who would be "believers," gathered as they were under the cloak of the tribes of Israel, for thousands of years before the exodus. After all, they were *already* Jews by the time they were enslaved in the land of Egypt. I believe that many had descended from the land of Ur, and had scattered throughout the lands. Some worked the water, at the ocean's side, while others toiled in the fields, especially at the foot of the great mountains."

"The history of the Jewish people is told in the Scriptures, a collection of historical writings, gathered from many sources, and over a great period of time. The Scriptures began as part of an "oral tradition," spoken aloud, and handed down through recitation, from father to son, until that time when they were finally written down, " said Moses.

"The Old Testament, which is the Bible that is used among the Jews, is itself a collection of books, which were collected under three main mantles. The first collection is called the "Torah," also described as the "Five Books of Moses," or the "Pentateuch". These five books include Genesis, Exodus, Leviticus, Numbers, and Deuteronomy. These stories tell of the origins of the world, as known to Man, and the process through which Man became enslaved. It describes the story of Man's regaining his freedom, at the hand of God; and, finally, there are a series of "divine instructions" which had originally been received as divine revelation.

"The second portion of the Old Testament contains the writing of The Prophets, starting with Joshua, and being completed by the later twelve prophets.

"That portion of the Old Testament which contains much of the poetry and which tells of the traditions of the Jewish beliefs, can be found in The Writings. It would be here that we find the Psalms, the Proverbs, the Story of Job, and so forth. Together, these books express our aspirations for understanding our God, and His workings."

"Hasn't there been some challenge to the possible authenticity of these Scriptures? I think that I heard someone say that they are each so different in style that they do not appear to be tackling the same questions?" I queried.

"As suggested, just a few minutes ago, the Scriptures are a *collection* of literature, which had originally been passed down by word of mouth; and, eventually, they were written in any one of various tongues of the people who had heard them. It is likely that the stories, which are told in the Old Testament, may have been variously translated into Latin, Hebrew, Arabic, Aramaic, Greek, and any of the ancient African tongues. It is derived from a diversity of cultures, and gathered over a few thousand years; and, possibly, on several continents. If it *had* appeared to have been of a single hand, I would have been greatly surprised."

This being said, Jehovah picked up a slate, and I could see that he was etching something on it with a stylus that he was holding. Then, he turned the slate around, so that I would be able to read what he had written. I had to admit that I had no idea what it said.

"And *that* is a secret that I've tried to keep to myself for millennia...My penmanship *stinks*! No wonder the peoples of the world have interpreted my many signs in so many different ways! I've had to work hard at getting my messengers to carry my message in a manner which might best be understood by their followers...Hey! You're not going to give away my secret, are you?"

"No, no. I think your secret will be safe with me. Besides, even if I ever tried to tell my story back home, I don't believe that anyone outside of my padded cell would even hear me."

To this, Moses added, "One does not question the existence of God; that is something which is simply an accepted truth to the Jewish people. What each man actively seeks in his study of religion is to understand the manner in which God acts in this world. I'm sure we've all heard that old statement, that God works in wondrous ways; well, that's why we are in search of some direction, since God does speak through *all things* in this world.

"He is the God of *all* peoples; so, all that talk heard about there being a "chosen" people, may seem to be confusing. But, if you think back a few minutes ago, to that story which Isis told, the one about her being separated into several parts, each with its own separate identity, but all still singularly the original, or Isis, then you may have a better understanding of what God really is. He is God to all of Mankind, but He may be known by various names, or identities. To Mog, down there, God may become significant through that stone figure he carries in his hand; He is the Mother Earth, the Giver of Life."

At this juncture in the proceedings, a figure from the Medieval Era stood up, and stepped forward. He had a puzzled expression on his face, and he was scratching his head.

"I've been meaning to ask...Why does this *primitive*," stated in a very condescending tone, "this one you call Mog, feature so prominently in everything which has been discussed thus far? After all, he has not even the intellect to comprehend our words, much less the depth of the thoughts being conveyed here. He is just a *savage*. He couldn't possibly make head nor tail of the Bible, even if he were held at the point of a sword."

This was truly a statement of the arrogance and presumed piety of the Medieval puritan movement in Western Europe. But, as these words were spoken, one could hear the sound of someone seemingly clearing his throat, though the sound came from far in the rear of the gathering. Beneath this faint sound, a puff of smoke could be seen rising, and slowly moving toward the center of the gathered circle present.

As I turned to look, and see who it might be, I noticed a slender man, with gray beard and hair, and smoking a rather large cigar. He stopped in his path, just in front of this gentleman that was questioning the significance of our friend, Mog. He took another puff from his cigar, and stated, in a rather thick Viennese accent, "Who are *you* to question the importance of another human being? In our discussion of the Old Testament, I believe that one is presented with ample evidence for the condemnation of the sin of *pride*, is there not? Because he cannot read, nor speak the same language as you, does this then mean that he cannot be saved? Is the Heaven, which we have been told of, to be understood simply as a sort of library, with our death certificate representing little more than a library card, which allows us to enter?

"I have always believed that *the child is father to man!*"

"So! What, exactly, is that supposed to mean?" asked our apparently arrogant snob.

"It means that, in *every* life, there is *first* the child. For Mankind, we might conceive of our undressed friend, there, as representing our infancy. The adult, with all of his logic and cognitive skills, and language, only arrives in this life at a later point in the cycle. However, as soon as one is confronted with a blindingly overwhelming question, or is faced with some insurmountable fear, one tends to seek out that very same *child*, wherever that child may be hiding deep inside."

"And, for what purpose?"

"It may well be that the time of the child in one's life was the only time when the magic of our thinking could make all things right again. There is *much* to be learned from that child."

He took another puff from his cigar, slowly approached Mog, and offered him a hand in friendship, and offered congratulations. Then he walked on.

Another of those assembled, of more recent date, disdainfully asked, "What the heck is Sigmund Freud doing among a group of deities? Who does he think he *is*?"

I noticed a wry smile, as Jehovah looked to Moses; and Jesus couldn't hold back his laughter. Jehovah turned to the man, and answered, "I can tell... You've never tried to be a therapist, have you?"

Everyone, except this one person, joined in the humor.

"Let's see, where were we? We were discussing the Old Testament, were we not?"

"Oh, yeh! Another question which often surfaces has to do with the temperament of God. For many of those, especially those in the Old School, God was always considered to be quite *severe*, and very *demanding*. He had given down his Commandments, and He demanded that they be followed precisely. Each and every violation would be written into the Book of Life, and one has but few opportunities in one's life to make good on these.

"However, it is to be noted that God is also *compassionate*. One may ask oneself if this is, in some way, a form of contradiction. Actually, what it represents is the very ambivalence which has always been a part of membership in Mankind, more than it is a part of God. Mankind's belief in God, in the first place, is a sign of Man's search for a state of "sanctuary". The tribes which became united under the Judaic faith were widespread; so, in its origins, the followers of the faith could settle on no permanent site for this sanctuary. Instead, this sanctuary was believed to be an *innate* place, born within each of us. As the people of Israel started to become more stable, the city of Jerusalem evolved as the permanent center for these people."

"But, isn't Judaism much like many of the polytheistic faiths which had gone before them? Are there not, then, a diversity of deities? In Christianity, one may note the elevation of certain human figures to the position of Sainthood. Are these figures not the subject, or object, of prayer?"

It was Joshua that rose, to answer this issue. "We, the Prophets, are to be conceived of simply as the "Spokesmen of the Faith". It is our mission to keep the spirit of God alive in Man. It would be far too easy for the practices of the faith to become so mechanical as to become *rote*, or insincere. The Prophets have come to Mankind at troubling times in the history of Man, for the purpose of once more adding vigor to their system of beliefs."

From the crowd, one hears "And what's all the to-do about this *Messiah*?"

"It was told to the Jews, through the process of the Revelations, that there would come a representative of God Himself, sent to help deliver the people into safety. It would be the Messiah that would clarify the path which Man was to follow. He would be an Anointed One, descended out of the House of David; and it would be He who would help break the yoke of oppression, which was holding Man."

"And just look how well you guys listened!" came another voice. "So, how come all the Jews weren't just *zapped* for that one great boo-boo; that really left you hanging out to dry...so to speak."

Jesus chose to field this one himself. "That was no walk in the park for me, I assure you, if you'll excuse the pun. But, in the end, I had to ask forgiveness for them. The part of the story that no one seems to hear, and the reason that so many malign the Jews, is that human nature has its flaws. Once it became known that the Messiah would be coming, there were all sorts of men, shaman and con men alike, who saw this as their way of, I guess you could call it, *turning a prophet*...Oy, sorry!! Another bad joke...After so many generations of fakers *appearing* at their door, each making claim to these powers, and some even offering up their own version of a "miracle," it became difficult for the Jewish people to believe *anyone* who made such claims. The Messiah would lead the people into a state of holiness, and out of the harshness, which was the reality of one's life on the Earth. However, these would-be Messiahs led the people only closer to the poorhouse."

"But, how could man be so flawed in this way? Wasn't he, too, a creation of this Perfect God?"

"I'm afraid that *that's* another question; and, maybe, we'll be able to answer that one...eventually. In the meantime, let's look at the fact that God handed down to man a system of laws and codes, which they were to follow. The first of these, of course, were the Ten Commandments, which were engraved by God's hand, on the stone of Mount Sinai. It was considered to be a gift to the Jewish people, who were in exodus from the land of the pharaohs. It was to serve both as a contract and a covenant with the people, and its purpose was to serve as the law of the land which they were then to inherit and work. The law, itself, possessed a duality, of being both civil and rabbinic law, where the church and the state were one.

"The exact *word* of God was not to be entirely and readily known to Man; the deeper meanings of The Word were things for which Man would have to seek, and delve into. Added to this was the Kabbalah, the Book of Traditions, which is perceived as the mystical writings of the law, and also a part of the Jewish belief system. It is through one's efforts at comprehending the teachings of the Kabbalah that each man may seek his own personal union with his God. It offers a series of spiritual exercises, meditations, and contemplations by which Man seeks a more spiritual process of personal growth. Similar processes of self-understanding and spiritual purification are also found among the Hindu, with the Tao, and within the study of Buddhism. For each, the goal appears to be similar, which is to "become one with the deity," through a process of cleansing and purification of one's own spirit.

"Among the Jewish people, there exists the belief that there is but the singular deity, that He is omnipotent and omnipresent, as well as all-loving. Under the tutorship of one's God, each man is created as a free agent, meaning that each man is born free, to seek and to follow, his own path. However, the path, which is open to man, is forever crossing between "good' and "evil," and there exists an ever-present temptation toward either direction."

After trying to digest this information, I was left with spaces to fill. "Are you then suggesting that, for those among Mankind, who are able to properly interpret God's word, I mean His meaning, that there will be some special favor granted? Just how, then, does God make His word known to Man?'

"God communicates to the living through the phenomenon of "revelation,"'" responded Moses, "which represents the "disclosure" of His meanings. In this same manner, God demands an obedience to His laws, as they have been expressed through the Torah. This, then, is the true path to an understanding of God's wisdom by the people of this Earth. And, through His word, we learn that it is the duty of each and every individual to live one's life in accord with the "Divine Will". In this way, one does not seek any promise of any type of "ultimate reward" as a motivation for seeking righteousness in this life. There is but the one path, which bears witness to God, and to His purpose in this world."

I thought for a moment, and again had to ask; "Doesn't that mean that, for those who are able to properly interpret God's word, there will be special favor?"

"No! On the contrary, *all* people are created equal in the eyes of God, no matter where they exist on the Earth, and no matter what it is they profess to believe. Each person is *precious* in the eyes of God. It is for this reason that God's plan has been established that each man's relationship with his fellow man should be like His own, and *that* relationship is based on *love*. In the Judaic tradition and beliefs, the greatest is "tsidaka," or *charity*. The manner in which each man treats his fellow man is one of the ways in which he demonstrates his belief in, and his love of, God."

"New Testament...Old Testament...the Koran...the Tao...It's all so confusing! So, what is the *true* way in which man may attain entry into Heaven? Isn't it true that Man's every effort in *this* world must be designed to gain placement in *that* next world? This seems to be what I've heard so much from religious leaders around the world. It's so important, that people are sacrificing their own lives in that effort at gaining glory for themselves and their ancestors."

"A good intent, which has been distorted to meet the design of a few...I would be hard-pressed to find any actual instructions which direct man to destroy the life which God himself has placed on this Earth.

"It is, rather, the goal of each man to properly, and fully, seek enjoyment in *this* world. But, in order for him to achieve this, it is important that the joy which man experience be something which may be *shared* by others. It is the welfare of society, as a whole, which is of the greatest importance; and this can be best promoted through the welfare of the family unit, which is the focal point of *all* belief. Jewish life has always focused on the home. It is within the home that the greatest, and the most important, learning takes place. The laws that govern Man's stay on the Earth have their roots in the home, and in the family. The most important of these laws are those of cleanliness, personal health, education, marriage, and diet.

The laws, as they are set forth, have been designed to direct one's life in this world, as well as to prepare one for eternity, as a form of purification."

"This is all true," stated Jesus. "And the Old Testament was one of the earliest written documents of any peoples, though it may have been written in many tongues, and over a length of time. What it represents is the story of a small, and relatively weak, nation, which had been frequently overrun by its more powerful neighbors. The Old Testament, after all, is so much more than simply a *religious* document; it is the actual *history* of a people. If one were to take a step back, and examine the Jewish people more carefully, one would be likely to discover a very *pragmatic* culture. Most of the rules for the operation of day-to-day activities were, in their original form, rules for managing one's health, one's education, and so forth."

Moses placed a hand on the shoulder of Jesus, and added, "If you require proof of this statement, let us just look at the laws which tell Mankind to maintain a Kosher home."

"While, in the modern era, one tends to view the maintenance of a kosher home as a "religious" practice, its original purposes dealt with the health rules. The kosher laws are designed as a protection of Mankind from scavengers, meaning those animals which survive on means other than grazing, and which often means their eating of unhealthy substances. Such animals are open to contaminants, *unless* one is fully aware of *all* that that animal feeds on. This is something over which Man may have some measure of control, as long as one controls the domestication and pasturing of these animals. Shellfish are not kosher, due to the fact that their exoskeleton, or shell, collects waste so inefficiently; as well as the fact that these animals are both scavengers, and bottom-feeders, that draw sustenance out of the ocean or stream bed.

"The Old Testament clearly presents the ways in which Man may be tested by God, in order that he is, in fact, a *moral* being. In the Book of Job, one examines the sin of "pride"...something that gentleman earlier seems to have overlooked when he attacked our friend Mog. While each man may readily be tempted in many ways in this life, each man is also capable of demonstrating strengths, as well as weaknesses. Job, while a prideful man, was also able to demonstrate the strength of "patience," and was able to submit himself freely to the will of God. By comparison, the heroes, who are presented in the Greek traditions and literature, appeared to be in a constant state of rebellion. Not only was Man constantly challenged, but even the gods would fight amongst themselves.

"The God of the Hebrews was known as everlasting. It was also believed that He lived *within* each of His believers. It was each man's job, then, to search inside of himself for his God. While the gods of the Greeks might often be considered to be fickle, the god of the Hebrews was always of certain purpose. It was considered important that each man keep God in his heart; and, for this reason, there was to be no representational images, or icons, of Him. Those who remained righteous, would be rewarded; but that reward might not be something immediate. Life is *eternal*, and one's rewards would eventually be granted."

As I looked about the gathering, I could see that there was a good deal of discussion initiated by this subject matter. Even Mog, who was still so excited at having been singled out for the special honors bestowed by Dr. Freud, seemed to be acting a bit more pensive...or, maybe, he was just getting bored with all of this talking. Whatever the reason, he seemed to be much calmer. And evening descended on this group once more.

I could hear stomachs starting to grumble, and the smell of fresh soup was in the air. Whoever was doing the cooking must have been cognizant of the facts presented in our discussion, for one could find no trace of either meat or seafood in the product being passed out for dinner.

However, along with the large bowls of soup, which were being distributed, there was a *huge* loaf of bread being passed around. Each of the deities, from the gods to the saints, to the demigods, would make some sort of blessing on the loaf, as they had upon their bowls, before partaking of the meal. Even Mog showed some constraint in the presence of the food, which, I would say, was one tremendous vote for what had been spoken to this point.

There was a decision made that, while the congregates were dining, there might be some form of "floor show," I guess one could call it. As this decision was made, several of the deities climbed to the top of a nearby hill. As they reached the summit, they could be observed making certain gesticulations, followed by a series of incantations, until the heavens seemed to come alive with "fireworks". There were fireworks in the form of shooting stars, and then there were the Northern Lights, an unusual occurrence this far south.

The gods of Nature offered a display of their own, in the form of a painting, using the leaves of the trees as their canvas, on which they painted the beautiful hues of the Fall. The wind was chanting a tune through the trees, which helped lull the audience into a trance-like state.

And, gradually, they even gave way to nightfall....and sleep.

Chapter Seven

There were many images drifting in and out of my mind, as I tried to sleep last night. While it was obvious to me that Man had indeed been able to come a long way since those days when all of Man was functioning at a level with our friend Mog, there really hadn't been any vastly dramatic changes in Man's beliefs at all. Man had always been aware that there had been *something* from which the world, as *we* knew it, had sprung forth...Well, "sprung" may not be the best of words for this phenomenon...But, then, again, I don't want to end up in any sort of Snopes trial, such as the one which placed William Jennings Bryant against that teacher, in the Old South.

That debate placed the "evolutionists" against the "Creationists," deep in the Bible Belt of the United States, and sought to control how American children would be taught about the beginnings of Mankind on the Earth. While Bryant was a conservative creationist, he was also a very political man. He was preaching that all life developed out of the cohabitation of Adam and Eve, in the Garden of Eden, directly interpreted out of the Old Testament. This argument was to decide whether or not the Old Testament would have to be presented as the absolute "text" for human history, or whether one might offer evidence which came out of the scientific laboratories, suggesting the possibility of an evolutionary path toward Mankind from the primates.

Modern society presents a plethora of alternative explanations, from the possible, to the exaggerated, to the absurd. In the movie, <u>Men In Black</u>, we are presented with a law enforcement agency, developed to manage and monitor those aliens from other worlds, already known to have arrived on the Earth. They are dealt with in a manner similar to the FBI's witness protection program, all kept from the awareness of the general population. The movie presents the case of a puzzle presented to the two detectives, which suggests that there is an entire universe which has disappeared, and eventually found in an orb, around the neck of one of the alien's pet cats. That's not so far fetched, is it!

If one were to take a few moments to study the structure which exists in our universe, one could start at the most minute of elements, and build one's field of study to encompass the largest units of our life. If one were to examine the single atom, one would find that there is a nucleus at its center, made up of a positively charged member, called a proton, around which are orbits of negatively charged electrons, moving around this nucleus. This entire equation is purposeful, and not simply sprung from nothing, without a plan. There is a balance to this whole equation, with the positively and negatively charged particles being of equal value, so that the orbits of the electrons do not become unstable. If one were to somehow remove one of these electrons from its orbit, which may occur at the outermost orbit, the atom would then seek to balance itself, to reach a state of equilibrium. This could possibly be accomplished by attracting an electron from a neighboring atom, from the outer orbit of *that* atom. If this is successfully accomplished, the result is *fusion*.

On the other hand, if one is seeking to *destabilize* the atom, one may bombard the atom with a high-energy field, attempting to knock one of the electrons out of its orbit. Again, this would cause the atom to seek a state of equilibrium, or balance; and the resulting event would be called *fission*.

Careful examination of these events would introduce us to an image which is familiar, indeed. The resulting structures are suggestive of the structure of our "universe". *Our* universe has the Sun at its center, which may be considered to be the nucleus, and there are planets, moons, and various satellites which orbit it. One finds that all the same forces which determine the structure and function of the smallest atom, also affect those collections of atoms, called "molecules". As one moves up the ladder of energy and matter, one finds that the same principles which govern the smallest particle, also serve the largest unit, such as our universe. The image, which comes to my own mind, is in the theme song from <u>The Umbrellas of Cherbourg</u>, which states "Like a wheel within a wheel...".

One also finds that the laws which govern the universe, may also hold true for the individual human being, in his daily struggle for existence. We, after all, are a physical mechanism, as well as a psychological organism, forever in search of a state of equilibrium. Let's look at the laws of physics. The "law of inertia" states that a body at rest will remain at rest, unless acted upon by some outside force. Inversely, a body in motion will remain in motion, unless acted on by some outside force, including gravity. The human organism is "motivated," or driven, by *needs, desires, urges, and drives*, which are internal reactions of the organism. These reactions may be innate functions, genetically determined and evolved, within the individual; or, they may have been *learned*, meaning that the reaction may be the result of the organism's experience in the world, and related to which behaviors have been rewarded. If the individual were to sense that, in some way, there were something lacking, something which could help one to feel complete, or satiated, the organism would then be motivated to formulate and act on some plan of action which might best satisfy that need or desire.

Of course, an obvious truth is that, for one to be able to function in this world, one must first *be in this world*. Therefore, we are faced with another of the great questions of Mankind, which asks how we arrived here in the first place. There would seem to have had to be some force, or entity, which had caused all life to be in the world in the first place. This may be the one universal concept which has been shared by the majority of religious beliefs in this world. As to what that power may be, or its purpose in doing so, *that* may not be so universally shared.

For Mog, and his friends, with the limitations set on them by their diminished cognitive skills, life may have appeared a bit simpler. Life has always been a matter of "survival" for them. But, even the simplest of creatures seems to be aware that there is a source to all life. Even the primitives...Sorry, Mog; no offense meant!...have witnessed the miracle of birth. And it was only logical for them to project this same understanding to the world which existed around them. Perhaps they had never observed the birth of a rock, nor been able to observe the gradual growth of a plant or tree; but, if these things actually existed *here*, on the Earth, then they had to have come from someplace.

For the early human-like organisms, then, the Earth must have been perceived as a giant "Mother". Life would germinate once a seed had been planted in the soil; and one could watch its growth. If this seed was properly nurtured, the plant would eventually break through the surface of the Earth, and reach toward the heavens for its sustenance, much as one sees among humans. The Cheyenne, a supposedly primitive Native American culture of the Southwest, perceived life in *all* of nature. Their ceremonies and rites always recognized the forces of Nature for its aid in their survival, and offered thanks.

And so, one might conceive of a few common themes in Man's belief systems. In the present congregation, one may note that, as Mankind socially and economically evolved, these beliefs and ideas had become more organized, and were written down. Thus, the initial form by which information and tradition were passed from generation to generation, that of oral tradition, was then augmented with the development of the written language.

As I looked around me, I noted that the congregation was again gathering, each group seeming to gather to itself. There had been an evolutionary unfolding to the presentations thus far, and I had no reason to believe that there would be change now.

As Mankind's physical and cognitive abilities developed, the way in which they perceived the world had changed, as well as the changes in their capacity to act on that world. The manner in which peoples organized their living and working groups, seemed related in some way to power relationships. The earliest organizational structure dealt with the nuclear family, as this was the size of the group which the economic system of the time could best support. From this, there evolved the extended family, the clan, the village, and then the city. Approximately at this same time in history, one comes upon the growth of the Roman Empire, with its tendrils reaching outside of Rome in an effort at bringing in, or, more factually, subjugating, the peoples around them.

It was within this Roman Civilization that one can first observe the finer art of organization, with the "institutionalization" of authority into some central governing entity. The Romans governed through a system of laws and codes, originally presented in Latin. This same system was then adapted for its use in the institutionalization of religion, too. Dissatisfied with his lot in life, the common man could seek some way of bettering his future, whether that would be here, on the Earth, or in another life. It was through religion that man sought the ultimate "equality"; all he had to do was to remain obedient to "the word," in *this* life.

I found that I had been voicing these thoughts publically, at least publically enough that some gentleman nearby could hear. He wore a flowing toga, and had an arrogant manner. He blurted out, "These rabble are just the scum of the Earth. One cannot govern an empire if one were forced to make consideration for *them!*"

Obviously, this was not one of the major gods of the Romans; and his manner suggested the lack of importance placed on him by his people. I soon discovered that this was, in fact, the orator, Cicero.

As he spoke, one could now hear the faint mumblings coming from the Christians, at least those predating Jesus himself. "Rome may have survived to this day if it hadn't have treated the common man more wisely. As with most human institutions, one could always find a pecking order, or hierarchy of power and influence. Those who possessed the social skills, and the education, usually suggesting that they were of noble birth, would gain their power by using those beneath them, as if they were rungs on a ladder.

"And, if this were not bad enough, the lowly peasant was made to feel indebted to his "superior" for the very little which he actually possessed. Is it not a fact that "aristocrats" would go so far as to free their slaves rather than accent the responsibility for feeding them? It was around the year 50 B.C., and these aristocrats applauded themselves for their humanitarianism; but it was evident to everyone that the real reason for their charity was purely financial. While the moneys were being spent in celebrating the community as a whole, none of this money ever made its way down the ladder to those who were really suffering, such as in the form of food. Is that not the true reason that Christianity gained in force among the people, in its renown as the freer of the downtrodden, as late as 180 A.D.?"

One of the Roman deities then rose, and, looking down at his feet, stated, "Yea, it is true that the Roman Empire fell, and with such great force that it would echo throughout history. It was a disease which begat the wealthy, who so unwisely bore their arrogance in public, for all the baser elements of society to witness. You see, the Roman economy had been based on slavery, on conquering and demeaning other peoples; and they would perceive themselves as being above the laws which had been established by these others. They had built the fortunes of Rome on the caches of the provinces, which they conquered.

"After all, it was Aristotle, the Greek philosopher, who had defined the art of war as being the natural art of "acquisition". It is evident that there was too great a focus on "things," with a lack of focus on the art of "being." The Stoic philosophies, which had preached a certain indifference to the pleasures of this world, believed that the slave and the freeman were equals; but this philosophy never grew to the point of becoming any sort of challenge to Roman ways of life. Instead, the dominant practice became that of piracy, and dealing in the sale of human flesh.

"But, such an economy, which is based on the free labor of slaves, had little to offer to the development of technologies, which is the force on which all economies grow. If one examines the dynamics of slavery, one finds very little which augments the productivity. There is little motivation on the part of the slave to produce more, and greater productivity for the slave owner only meant an investment in more slaves. It was Aristotle, once more, who had suggested that it would not behoove the average citizen of Rome to learn the crafts, which had been practiced by his "inferiors".

Thus, the farming of the land could be conceived of as the most noble source from which a man could accumulate wealth, so long as he did not have to toil in it himself. I believe that, had Jesus, or Moses, or Jehovah, come upon this scene, it is most likely that each would have perceived those, who had been born to slavery, as being the purest of heart, and thus were more likely to earn the rewards of the spirit. After all, was it not said that "the meek shall inherit the Earth"?

"And so, the Romans actively resisted the advent of any technologies, and, with it, economic improvement. In reality, this process served to minimize the value which might be placed upon the land itself; and placing the greater emphasis on the labor, over which the Roman, himself, did not personally invest. What it did, was to necessitate an expansion of slavery.

"For the most part, the majority of the citizens of Rome were never to have tasted the fruits of their labors. In the end, the process resulted in the Revolt of Spartacus, which lasted from 73 to 71 B.C. Worse yet, the process of war had become another economic necessity, for this was the only way of expanding the labor force. This led to another thought, which modern man cannot be proud of, and that is that no one wishes to feed a peacetime army. While they are at war, the soldiers can fend for themselves. At peace, Rome would become like a body which was gnawing off its own foot in order to survive.

"This process seemed to become a never-ending spiral. Once there were more slaves to work the lands, there was again the need to feed them; and this demanded a greater cultivation of the land...and, more slaves. I believe that there has been presented the prophetic observation, "Oh! What fools these mortals be!"

"It would appear that the commoner was in search of a philosophy which could offer some measure of comfort to daily life, as well as being a source of inspiration...something which could challenge, or displace, that philosophy which preached that Man was simply a witless victim of fortune and chance in this world. That victim of whim would have to be content with whatever might come his way."

Just then, there rose another of this ancient group. He had been sitting patiently till then, rubbing his beard, and considering the conversation. "The supreme virtue, indeed, could not be wealth, but *reason*. It could only be through the passage of reason that one would be capable of attaining a more expanded concept of life, and one which has no great barriers to bind it. It would be the task of Man to subjugate, *not* his fellow man, but his *passion*, in order that reason could thrive. One could find this same process approaching its strength in the Sixth Century B.C., in Greece, where the philosophy of Orphism preached of the uselessness of this life on Earth. Accordingly, this system expressed the belief that one's sole purpose in this life was to seek redemption for one's sins, and an apology for one's human frailties.

"Those spiritual beliefs, which predated the Christian Era, offered praise to a maternal spirit, a saving deity with whom the individual sought to *unite*. In this way, it appears similar to Dr. Freud's observation regarding the manner in which the individual might function under extremes of stress, such as forming a fetal ball, in some attempt at gaining the security which one once experienced only in the womb, a total return to one's original source of life. The Sybylline Oracle, of Asia Minor, had preached of the "Rites of the Great Mother". Among the Persians, one found the existence of a spirit, named Mitra, that was exalted, and the praise was demonstrated in the form of the sacrifice of a bull. Among the Egyptians, Isis was praised as the "Mother of the Heaven and the Gods," which also expressed a concept of unity of power.

"As we have already heard, Judaism evolved through a system of Scriptures. While one tends to find that many religious systems have as their goal the bringing of others into their beliefs, the Jewish people believed that their demonstration of their faith would be sufficient to demonstrate to man how one might best profit spiritually, and that the faith would naturally spread in this way, without a need for seeking conversions by force. It is, at least in part, for this reason, that the Jews segregated themselves from as much of the strife of the outside world as they could. Within the civilized populations of the world, one found that the Jewish people gathered together, and formed ghettos.

"Most have the belief that it would be impossible to escape the potential of at least some suffering in this life; it is inevitable and inescapable. It would be one's own faith which would serve as the tool which makes this life tolerable, and which enables one to purify oneself for one's entry into the next life. For the Jewish people, even their deity, Jehovah, remains a

117

remote figure. It is believed that He resides in the heart, and in the mind. For other civilizations of the time, such as the Greeks, the deities were believed to exist as neighbors to Man. However, even in this distinction, between being *of this world*, and being *an ethereal force*, it was Christianity which served to bridge this gap. Accordingly, Jesus, the Christ, had made it His *choice* to take this earthly mantle, and to offer His sacrifice in the name of His fellow man. He willingly accepted mortality, and thus, was of *both*, the mortal, and the ethereal."

As I listened to these various conceptions of Man, it became obvious that the philosophies of Man share more than they differ. The three major schools of thought, Judaism, Christianity, and Islam, all had a common origin; and, even those, who were to be considered as Christians, identified *themselves* as being Jews, who had initially followed the Old Testament. Islam, too, was born of the Old Testament, which then merged into the Koran, after the birth of Mohammed.

The Romans found that a belief in a singular God was a danger to their way of life, and challenged the Caesars as themselves being deities, applied pressure to the Jewish people. As deities, the Roman emperors used their skills as manipulators of humanity to set one belief against another, in an attempt at weakening the old beliefs.

By the First Century B.C., Judaism was developing two factions, the Sadducees and the Pharisees, the first being the more conservative, while the second was more accepting of progressive thinking. For the Jewish people, life was not considered to be totally a sacrifice in the name of a potential glory in the hereafter, but something which was to be enjoyed while on Earth, as a gift from God. This did not mean that Man should be tolerant of negative influences on his beliefs; Man was imbued with a gentleness, and a loving kindness, which would help him to be his brother's keeper, that he might better share that goodness.

Prior to the development of Judaism, one could find the Cult of Isis, as well as the Cult of Mithra, both in Persia. Isis served as a mothering god-figure, who was mystically linked to the past through a series of miracles. The Cult of Mithra prophesied a future life for Man; but this was never a well organized system. Mithra was seen as mediating between those who lived on Earth, and the gods in the heavens.

The development of Christianity seemed to encapsulate enough of the previous belief systems so that it might feel "comfortable" and "familiar" to the common man, while it preached that Mankind must not seek the excesses in life. One would find peace through the living of a quiet life, faithful to the Christian ideal. It adopted the concept of immortality, which was prominent in Egypt at the time, as well as among the Greeks, and the Hebrews. Christianity was presented as a Neo-Platonic philosophy, which would perceive of this world as merely an imperfect reflection of an ideal, which would exist in Heaven alone.

Christianity did not openly accept the habits of the more "pagan" systems of belief; however, it seems to have been able to "tame," and then extend them, in a process of religious "rites," which served to bring the people together in prayer. It was able to accept some of the more naturalistic rites of the previous practices, mimicking them, and, in this way, found a greater acceptance among its followers. If one were to study such cultures as the Druids, one might find some similarities to the Christian Church today, such as the celebration of seasonal festivals, which we find in Easter. Easter has been described as a celebration of the resurrection of Christ; but it also represents a form of harvest festival seen in many other cultures.

That which was formulated from this early Christian period was a style of life, which was to be known as "the Christian Way of Life," a means by which man could attain entry into the next life, in Heaven. This process was a mixture of the practical with the ideal; the sensual with the ascetic. The human body was perceived as imperfect, possessing certain weaknesses, which the Christian path could purify.

Man could not trust the flesh, for the flesh was weak, and could lead him astray. This, above all things, may have led to the greatest contradiction to be found in the faith. If Man was, indeed, created in the image of God, and his human form was a gift from that God, then it is something which Man should cherish, serving as his temple. However, at the same time, it is readily recognized that this "gift" may be flawed. While it is the vehicle, and the vessel, which was given by God, in which to harbor the soul, it yet demanded the diligent work of man to prepare that soul for that next step, seen in its rise to Heaven. The Bible states that, without Divine Intervention, Man would naturally be turned toward the wicked. The cults, which preceded modern Christianity, processed that Divine Intervention through the use of "totems," or symbols of the Earth to which the individual could turn for guidance.

Of all the sins known to Man, the greatest was considered to be Pride, which was conceived of as a form of self-satisfaction, a form of self-indulgence, which detracts from the praise he could offer to God for our gifts. The sensible man would be he who seeks moderation in all things worldly. He is wise who is unselfish, and who seeks his own salvation through his efforts for Mankind. The unity of Mankind becomes a much greater reward than is personal triumph.

There was a silence, for just a moment, and once again, one could make out a faint puff of smoke rising at the periphery of the gathering, but the figure remained out of sight for the moment. Finally, one could hear someone clearing his throat, and then, in a strong Viennese accent, he said, "I believe that this is one of the topics which I have covered myself; and some of my...pardon the expression..."disciples," such as Drs. Adler and Jung, have lent their support to these thoughts.

"I believe that this, which you have mentioned, could be conceived of as the expression of the "self" in the process of one's life, and it becomes the function of the "ego". The ego is one of the entities of the personality which mediates between the strongly instinctual "Id," and the severely moralistic "Superego". I believe that it was Dr. Jung who extended this concept as relating to the deeper social and anthropological inheritance of Mankind. Dr. Jung has described a portion of the personality in which all of Man's heredity, from his first steps on the Earth, would be stored, and which was molded by each and every experience in his life, as a means of improving man's social functioning. As for myself, I identified this more primitive aspect of the total self, a part from which the more socially appropriate self would emerge, as "das ich," meaning the "I"; however, through its translation into English, when I was first introduced to America, at Clark University, it became known as the "Id".

"Once more, I would like to refer to our robust friend there, Mog, as an organism who is more fully motivated by that primitive self, which may be found in the Id. If one were to remain constantly in that particular state of development of the self, one would then function predominantly at the level of the instinct, a more aggressive manner of functioning if it were left unchecked. I believe that it may be at this level which some become fixed in their development, and have been institution-alized as a means of protecting both them, and society.

"As we witness the evolution of civilization, we note the development of the extended family, and then, the clan; and, with that development, there also evolved the need for a greater level of cooperation amongst men. This, of course, would mean that one's personal goals and drives might have to be inten-tionally curbed, set aside, or restrained in order that the good of the group be considered. That term, which I have found to be most relevant to that part of the self involved in these types of controls, would be the "conscience," often defined as the urge to do right, and thus demanding that there also exists a differentiation between "right" and "wrong".

"Und, now maybe, we have discovered the entry-point for the development of Christian beliefs. It is through its defini-tion, and its emphasis on, "right and wrong" that Christian thought gains its force among peoples. The establishment of the "Church," as an institution, is based upon the development of the superego within each man, a molding of that portion of the human brain/mind which controls behavior, and which enables man to survive in the social setting. However, should the superego become excessively dominant in the personality, the result would be punitive reaction against the self, which would be so limiting to the individual as to destroy the self. Und, so vee see, that the Church, which has been formulated as an institution which might best help us seek that balance between the instinctual needs of the organism, and the con-trols which are necessary for life among one's fellow man, would be the most effective source of managing social power.

"It was in America, I believe, that a number of communal sects developed, with philosophies which were strongly fo-cused in the direction of superego superiority, and thus, the control of human desire. There remain religious groups which continue to advocate such stern controls, and have sometimes been looked upon as delightfully naïve, if not totally unrealistic ideals. The considerations of these groups was to find some means of cleansing the mind and body of the "unclean," of sin, through the negation of the sensual pleasures from life. In so doing, this ban also denied the potential for the reproduction of the species; and the future of these groups depended on being able to constantly attract outsiders to join its membership. Needless to say, few humans have been seduced by these demands for sacrifice; und so, these communities have failed to thrive.

"Within the formal organization of the Christian Church, there have been similar, isolated communities, which attempted a similar devotion and cleansing of the soul. There are the Convents, and Monasteries, and retreats established for the purpose of purifying one's spirit. But, even here, one cannot avoid notice of the flaws which exist in the human vehicle which carries the soul. While they certainly remain devout in their beliefs, there are many who have taken the vows, who have discovered that they could not successfully fend off the demands which their bodies make upon them."

Jehovah approached Dr. Freud, and extended His hand as a sign of His appreciation for this exposition on how Christianity could be explained through this more practical, earthly focus.

One of the Disciples of Christ then rose. "Christianity most certainly recognizes those weaknesses which are Man's. There has always been a certain distrust for the kind of thinking which might distract even the best man from his path to salvation. And yet, we also find that neither is the purest from of "rationalism" acceptable, perceived as a severely *factual* manner of thinking, much as one would find coming from the character of Spock, that member of the <u>Star Trek</u> crew...not the doctor, please. Any cognitive process, which is purely rational in content, would tend to undermine any potential belief in the *supernatural*. Remember, we have asked Man to believe in a force which cannot be sensed with his Earthly senses alone. It is through one's *faith*, alone, that *certainty* can be measured. Christianity serves as a seeker after perfection; but this process is performed while one resides in an imperfect world. This, then is Man's true **"test of faith"**."

"This discussion appears to have taken a turn toward the New Testament, which, historically, would begin with The Sermon On The Mount. So, please pardon my intrusion here, but I believe that, perhaps, I, Paul, as a disciple of Jesus, and the man who witnessed his word, could best present these principles.

"As one of the Apostles, I was one of the many who helped in writing the Scripture, which were to become the New Testament. As a matter of fact, it was Matthew who was present at the site, and who recorded the Sermon.

"Those of us who were witness to the words of Jesus knew that our faith would be drawn in new directions, a turn from the "Lord Who Was To Be Feared". In the Book of Acts, the history of the founders of the faith is presented, which also presented some organizational suggestions for the structure of the institution of the Church. It was presented as a message of salvation, to be offered to Jew and Gentile alike. It became my personal mission to pass these teachings along to the masses. I attempted to organize this material into some sort of consistent doctrine, something which Man might find easier to follow. I talked about such things as original sin, of predestination, or election, and of grace.

"I found that the Old Testament had left people feeling callous, and frail. They were seeking some way of reconciling with their faith. This, I found, could be accomplished through the New Testament. In this document, the rules have been presented so that one may reconcile issues amongst one's brethren, as the initial step in their direction toward preparing any sort of gift, to be set before one's God. The Old Testament was, indeed, harsh; and it preached of distrust. The New Testament was designed to preach a love of one's fellow man, as well as a love of one's enemies. God should be perceived as a source of compassion, and it is Man's mission to seek similar strengths in himself. It may be in this manner that Man has been made in God's image."

This certainly was confusing for anyone who was seeking to determine his faith. The two Scriptures were so much alike; yet, they were so different. What could be the reason for this vast change from the Old to the New, from the book filled with *rage*, to the teachings of *love*?

Evidently, my puzzlement had not been so private, and Jesus put a hand on my shoulder, as he said, "I see how perplexed you appear to be over this, that the word of God, spoken as it is in these two places, would appear to be so different. Well, perhaps it is well that you ask, even if it be silently.

"It is important to remember that the Old Testament had emerged from the most primitive of human condition, and from an area of the known world which present-day scientists believe to have been the source of all human life on this planet...the Fertile Crescent, the Tigris-Euphrates Valley, Mesopotamia. Life was most certainly harsh, and survival uncertain. It was a matter of a daily struggle for survival in a very un-giving land. One finds a certain human trait that, when Man seeks change of some sort, he also tends to *overcompensate*, often demanding the opposite extreme. And, it appears that this may have been the situation in the preparation of the Scriptures.

"It was in the Old Testament that one finds the presumption that Man possessed the potential for *perfection*, which represents Man's image of what he believes God would have been; after all, was not this the model from which Man was said to have been molded? And, God's word was to be obeyed *to the letter*, lest one suffer His wrath.

"However, once God looked upon the face of the Earth, and He observed the condition of that which He had made, and noted they had wandered from the path He had set, He made the decision to send His only son to live among them, **as one of them**, in hopes that He could return Man to the paths of righteousness, and to remind them of His laws. One must remember that the vehicle which was used for this mission would be the *human body*, in the form it had always been available to every human on the Earth, from the beginning of recorded time.

"In this Earthly mantle, I grew intolerant of that which I was to witness among the mortals; and, even I expressed my *rage* openly, in the marketplace...and it was I who used my Father's name in vain. The Old Testament, which was still firmly in place over the people, clearly stated that *anyone* who was guilty of these imperfections would have to suffer God's wrath. And so, I was placed in the hands of the mortal courts, as were other men; and His justice had to be played out.

"However, from this, one had to consider that at least some part of the responsibility for Man's divergence from the straight-and-narrow path would have to rest in the workings of that machine, the human body, itself; and this was the vehicle which God had created as the cradle of each man's soul on Earth. Being now aware of the pains which this may have caused to

Mankind, one finds the New Testament branching out into new directions, and presenting the loving and forgiving Father, who demonstrates tolerance toward Man, in his search for the path to righteousness."

"Gee! That certainly makes *me* feel some sense of relief. It helps me to see that God may be willing to at least expect from Himself that which He has demanded from us. Leniency is a great virtue, as it's expressed in the courts, whether they be the mundane, or the spiritual."

You can bet that life would certainly feel easier, and we might even seek some measure of that perfection, if we knew that our little errors and blunders wouldn't be used against us in the final judgment.

As these thoughts passed through my mind, I realized that the hour was getting late, and I still had much to work through in my head.

Just then there was a commotion in the bushes, at the end of the gathering. Sure enough, I could see Mog; he was beating the bushes, foraging for something to eat. When Mog got restless, those around him also kept their wits about them, not wanting to become a part of the main course.

Night slowly descended on this congregation. The day had witnessed the development of an "institutionalization" for its belief systems, a form of organization which could focus towards a specific, and unified, purpose.

What still remained, was a question of whether this "institution" actually represented an expression of God's word, or whether it was merely a means by which Man could manipulate His words, and, in doing so, manipulate other men!

Chapter Eight

Once dinner had been enjoyed, all settled back in their seats in order to absorb the calm of these surroundings, and to enjoy one another. All had, by now, developed a greater understanding of the condition of Man in the universe, as well as his relationship to the deities. It was clear that one could not know Man, without knowing his beliefs and desires, which then involved the spiritual side of Man. It was also clear that that which Man had been seeking from his deity was in the process of evolution, much like the old saying,

The more we know we know,

The more we know we don't know.

In the beginnings of Mankind, there existed *needs*, defined as the requirements for the physical survival of the organism, and the species as a whole. For the human, when one is evaluating needs, one must take into account *both* the individual's *perception* of that which he may presently possess, and that which he *desires*, or wants. In this light, we find that a need is something for which there may be clear measurements.

With the evolution of human life, and with the advances in technologies, Mankind found that less and less of his time had to be focused directly on the immediate demands for survival.

He was left with time, and with the skills, with which he might seek *beyond* mere survival, or needs, and be capable of seeking after those things which may be better defined as *wants*.

Along with this evolution from needs to wants, there also followed a change in the manner of Man's interactions with his deities. While the more primitive homo sapiens were bound to a more concrete cognitive ability, with evolution, Man was developing *abstract* cognitive capabilities. Man could think beyond the tangible and immediate; he could *imagine*, or develop mental images based on thought and feeling, which could delve into areas extending beyond mere survival. The ability to *examine* that which one possessed allowed Man to develop an appreciation for the *qualities* of his existence; and this opened his thinking to a search for a sense of "meaning" and "purpose" in his life. It allowed one to think of "life" itself, rather than simply stumbling forward in the control of fate.

What is even more significant was the fact that Man could now *think about thinking*, which became the one consideration which raised Mankind's capacities above that of the common beasts of the field.

And, with these thoughts in minds, it was not surprising that one could detect new voices within the crowd. One of these, a rather grim figure, dressed in black, his face shrouded from view, rose and addressed the congregation. He identified himself as the embodiment of the Bubonic Plague, the Black Death, which occurred in Europe around the year 1348 A.D.

"Aye, 'twas I who brought Europe to her knees. And 'twas I who forced that great test of faith for all who identified themselves as Christians. There was no man alive who knew from whence I came, whether it was bourn on the wind, whether alive in the vicutals, or simply a curse from the Unholy.

"Ha! But I served Man well. I gave him a legitimization for all those behaviors which allow one to seek after satisfaction of one's appetites. The Church was, indeed, sorely pressed to provide answers, to provide succor to those so distressed. But, as man could see that the end of life might truly be at hand, at a time that he felt he was receiving no real comfort from the Mother Church, he might then seek after that comfort where else he could.

"The Church was preaching of brotherly love; but one might be able to observe that the only certain avoidance of this horrible fate could be found in *escape*. The question remained, however, of how to escape that which one could not see! Would there not be the fear that, in this escape, he would not simply be carrying the death with him to that next place?...And carry it, he did...Ha-ha-ha!

"As a result of *my* small successes, the Church was no more united as before, and the solidarity of the family would suffer as well. There were those who would even abandon their own children in the face of the death should they have remained where they were. Of all the storage set aside as insurance against times of famine, little was left. There was a radical halt to productivity, since this concept, in itself, demands a conception of "a future," which no longer existed."

Seeking equal time, I noticed another of this era, but one with a saintly glow, who would offer testimony here.

"Certainly, there was chaos; but those who did survive, and who managed to amass some measure of pliable wealth, were able to gain the greatest of honors within European society. Once in power, that sin, of *pride*, could find even greater support. The raging of the common man, the humble man, was great indeed, fed even more by the public executions in the town squares, replacing their need for food with a feeding of their hatreds. Art portrays realities, as one may find in such novels as Germinale and A Tale of Two Cities.

"Those who were able to rise in the aristocracy did so by the process of amassing material wealth, and not by any power of intellect, or their piety. While intellect was not the major consideration for leadership, it is also true that society relied on those with the greater education for advice on matters of state, or finance, which placed reliance squarely upon the clergy, in which the seat of education rested. The Church possessed power; but the clergy, themselves, did not have complete control over their own psychological "gremlins"...and thus, it was always a possibility that, with whatever knowledge they might provide, could also come any of those deeper psychological weaknesses, which distort reality.

"For those who found themselves in positions of leadership at this time, were the threats of violent sentiment from those they led, from their own pride, and from their awareness of the power which could be thrust upon them. All of this served to manipulate them, and they were intoxicated by it. While they could state that their function was in the name of "justice," their action might more likely have been in response to their desire for revenge; and they believed that their endeavors were blessed by the Church. The Church, at this time, had been sponsored by the royal court of the lands in which they existed. There could be no such concept as "leniency" toward Mankind, though this is what was advocated in the New Testament, by which the Church was supposedly ruled.

"The Church, in Europe, was dominated by a distant power in Rome. The distance of which I speak is not only in miles, but in customs, in language, and in economics. The Church in Rome shared very little with those who actually existed under its influence.

"The socio-economic setting of Medieval Europe was that of a feudal-manorial system, in which the lord of the manor existed as the only one who possessed privilege. He completely dominated the culture, and even *owned* the peasants who existed within his domination.

"The Medieval European Church was also of this design. The Church, in Rome, represented the Church Father, while the bishops and abbots, among whom the properties of the Church had been distributed, each served as the lord of his manor. With this hierarchical structure in place, even the "Lords" of the Church might gain power through the practice of "purchasing privilege".

"While modern Man cherishes an idealized image of the clergy, as being pure of heart and action, and bound by the strictest of admonitions against succumbing to the weaknesses and frailties of the body, the early Church was in no way established on such policies as abstinence, or vows of poverty. Indeed, the Church was itself a feudal state, and its lords could marry, and could possess lands, which could then be handed down through the generations to their progeny.

"And, as his title suggested, the Pope was "The Defender Of The Faith," and served as a war-lord, whose job it was to lead the army of the Church against any intruder. In this process, he would subjugate the peoples of these various lands, confiscate their property, and would take slaves and concubines into his possession. While most of the wealth which was thus gained would be transferred to the Church in Rome, in the form of "tribute," the rest might be invested in the fiefs, or inheritable properties, which then controlled the laymen within its boundaries.

"Only further corruption could come of such an arrangement, which eventually led to decay within the Church. As the power of the Church slowly leaked into the local Fiefs, the obedience which they had, to that point, showed to the central Church, in Rome, also began to erode. As a result, there was a loss in Papal authority and prestige. The Church had become so engrossed in the Earthly accumulation of wealth and power, that, by the Tenth Century, it was forced to focus so much less on its religious leadership and spiritual perspective.

"That gap, between Christian "ideals" and common Christian "practices," had been widening. Up to the year 1059 A.D., the College of Cardinals, in Rome, had been empowered as the overseer of all Church practices. It was also the body which then made the decision that those who accepted the robes of the clergy would now, and ever after, remain "chaste," explaining that the confusion created by getting mixed in the mire of the mundane, such as family matters, or property, could cloud one's mind with worldly thoughts and interests, and thus, distract him from the "otherworldly".

"Much of this was an effort at refocusing the clergy toward the work of shepherds, leading their flock toward their heavenly goal. In this process, the monasteries developed relatively independent rule, and offered support to the arts and to science. However, the monasteries were certainly no stranger to the production of real goods, as anyone who has ever quenched a thirst with Benedictine brandy might attest. The brothers and friars, such as those of the Franciscan, Dominican, and Jesuit Orders, served society as educators, as well as being a primary source of some rudimentary "social work".

"By this time in history, Europe was turning the corner on the Renaissance; but, prior to the teachings of such scientific minds as Copernicus, the Church had conceived of Man as being the "center" of the universe. What evolved from this type of thinking was a very materialistic philosophy, with a sense of self-indulgence, and the development of power politics. Those with a more ethereal bent could no longer tolerate the contamination of the Church in this way. The Renaissance Church evolved in reaction to those very same mortal sins of pride, anger, and covetousness, which had developed through the Middle ages. With this revolt, there came the revival of classical wisdom, with greater exuberance, as found in Greek philosophy and literature."

There is a rustling in the crowd, and someone steps forth. "I believe that *I* might be able to take over from here."

"Who is *that*?" I queried.

"Some guy named Luther."

"Luther *Who*?"

"Not Luther Who...Martin Luther!"

"Oh. I see."

And thus, he continued. "I never expected that there would be such a to-do over my simply posting those "Ninety-Five Theses" on the door of the chapel, at the University of Wittenberg. It was October 31, in the year of our Lord 1517, and the very eve of All Saints' Day. At the time, I was employed as a professor of divinity at that school, and I had only meant those statements to be a challenge to the faculty, for the purposes of a debate, which had already been scheduled to take place.

"I had, you see, joined the Order of Augustin Canons, simply as a challenge to the problems which I had been experiencing within my own faith. Instead of offering me strength, as I had hoped, it only further convinced me of my unworthiness for salvation. It was through the Diet of Spires that the protests were formally raised among the German priests, as a cry against the practices of the Church in Rome. I believe that *that* became the source for the term "Protest-ant," which later became a force of its own in European thought and belief.

"What I was seeking in this process was some sort of response from the Church as to why it afforded "indulgences" to sinners, just so long as they could afford some remunerative arrangement with the Church fathers. Those who had protested these practices believed that one should rather ask forgiveness directly from God, rather than through the Church hierarchy. It is, after all, only through the glory of God that one may attain redemption. It is through one's *faith* that one may find salvation, and not through the performance of corporal works. I believe that every man serves as his own priest; but I realize that this statement, if widely accepted, might affect the power which was then held by the clergy."

"So, how were you received?" I asked.

"Would you believe, Pope Leo X excommunicated me from the Church, which, I guess, he felt was necessary after I burned that Papal Bull, back in 1521. I'm afraid that my teachings were condemned as heresy by the Church. I guess that it was my mistake to attack the power of the Church because it was my belief that one's religion was solely a matter between the individual and his Creator. There existed little need for an institutional hierarchy, if my beliefs were held; especially since, at each tier of that hierarchy, some form of tribute was expected. It is through one's own efforts that the individual is capable of determining his own ultimate salvation...or, if the contrary be true, his damnation.

"We may see this theme most clearly portrayed in the legendary tale of Dr. Heinrich Faust, or Faustus, depending on the version which you read. The actual character of the Faust figure has historical merit, and grew out of the Middle East. It was popular, at the time, for scholars to travel throughout the civilized world, seeking to augment their own knowledge, in science and the humanities. Of course, a learned figure, out of the Middle East, dressed in foreign garb, and filled with knowledge and ideas which were as yet well beyond the northern Europeans, who were only recently out of the ancient ways of life, would raise an eyebrow or two.

"The tale of Faust tells of an individual, who actively seeks to possess *all* of the wisdom of Man. To this end, he is willing to make a deal with the dark forces. It is a sign of his arrogance to believe that, once he indeed possesses this knowledge, he will most certainly possess the ability of outwitting the Devil. The prize, of course, is Man's immortal soul.

"In the Medieval version of this legend, Faust, of course, is damned to Hell, for even thinking he could attain this sort of power. In the Renaissance version, however, and with his last breath, he simply asks God for salvation, and two angels descend to carry him to Heaven.

"Among my followers, I am most certain that there would be agreement that all *men*, at heart, are sinners. This is an accepted truth. The Old Testament describes the original sin, in the Garden of Eden; so, Mankind's roots have grown from this soil. However, it is *another* truth which states that what one assesses in Man is his *faith*, which is a gift that is granted to each man directly from his Creator.

"And so, we find that there are four areas in which I diverge from the Church in Rome. First, I believe that man may be saved through his faith, and not through his works or through the tribute which he pays. Second, the true authority of any religious belief rests in the word of God, and not in any arbitrarily developed institution, which is but a creation of Man. Third, the Church, as a living thing, is not a "structure"; it is, rather, a community of Christian believers. And, finally, the essence of a Christian life may be found in one's service to God, and not in serving the Church."

There is suddenly a voice from nearby. "I agree with most of what you have stated; but I don't believe that you have gone far enough in your castigation of the institutional degradation of the Church."

Luther turns, and asks, "Who is in question of what I say?"

"It is I, John Calvin."

"Ah. So, what have you to offer?"

"I grant your discomfort with the Church, but I do not believe that you are puritanical enough, Martin. There has been far too much of the mundane which has been filtering into the Church; we must apply pressure to seek an austerity, and punish those who seek power and glory for their own selfish reasons. After all, it is God, alone, who is all-powerful; and each of our fates has already been predestined as we first step upon the Earth. The sins of Adam were *unpardonable*, and we must each pay a price for the deeds of every other sinner before us. It is only through God's grace that one may find salvation."

I thought I was thinking to myself, but I guess I was actually speaking this out loud; "Wow! He's a little harsh, wouldn't you say!"

Luther leaned toward me, cupped his hand to his mouth, and whispered, "Wait, I don't think he's finished. There's bound to be more."

And, he was correct. "*All* wisdom can be partitioned between that which is a knowledge of God, and that which is a knowledge of *self*. But, above all, it is the task of each man to learn *humility*, and that all praise must be given to God, alone, for the gifts which we enjoy. God is the only "perfection". Mankind is depraved, he is poor, he is infirm, he is vane, and he is corrupt. All that Man is capable of seeing in himself is a vane appearance of righteousness. As we are each created in His image, then, by the right of creation, we are each subject to His authority!"

I was still swallowing hard from the previous statement. "Man, he doesn't beat around the bush, does he? Well, I guess that it's a refreshing change to hear someone who can put it right on the line. It certainly leaves little room for any errors in interpretation.

Chapter Nine

Well, just as I thought I had heard it all, at least in terms of such a very moralistic and intense belief system, I could hear some rustling down to my right, as a tall, bearded gentleman rose, and took the floor. He wore a headdress of checkered cloth, which was held to his head by a band of banded black rope. His robe was white, with some scrollwork along the neck area. I was seated at the fire's edge, and the heat was becoming intense. I wiped by brow, and reached, to take a sip from the chalice which rest in front of me. Finally, this figure spoke.

"You will please excuse me for my intrusion, but I have heard so much about the followers of the Christ, from the Children of Israel, and from the revelers of the Earth-Mother; we may be among the most recent arrivals amidst the world's most populace beliefs, but, I believe, this would be an opportune moment to present our own views."

"Who's that?" I asked.

"That, my friend," said Jehovah, "is Mohammed, of the Kuraish Clan."

"I have labored for generations over the confusion in which the world has held my teachings. Are they not much the same as those of the followers of Jehovah? We are both of Semitic ancestry; and both have their origins in the Old Testament. However, as Christianity diverged after the Sermon on the Mount, and passed its wisdom on through the New Testament, we, of the Islamic faith, followed another path, with the writings of the Koran.

"Following the domination of this area of the Middle East by the Greeks, the Semitic peoples took from that culture that which would be amenable to life in this area of the world, and they absorbed it into their own cultures. It is a fact that Islam emerged out of Byzantine Neo-Platonic Christianity, and from the lore of Ioaseph, who was the son of a king of India. This lore was then further refined through the Tales of Barlaam, who was a monk who had passed these stories on into the land of Persia; and later, they were passed into the lands of the Caucasus, in that area which lies between the Black and the Caspian Seas. It was first translated into an Indian tongue, one in which Ioaseph was given the name of Boddhisattva. And it was through *this* translation that the legends speak of a Christian Saint.

"The word Islam, itself, is an Arabic term, which means "submission". I had no intention of establishing any such following. I was born of simple stock, to a poor clan, around 570 A.D., and was orphaned at a very young age. I was raised by relatives, and later became the servant of an older female of the area. It was my ability to manage her properties which most impressed her, to the point that we were later to wed. We prospered through the wise management of her properties, and our holdings quickly expanded.

"I was asked to travel, on behalf of that estate; and I was able to gain a familiarity with the beliefs and the cultures of the peoples within my own realm, as well as the surrounding areas. I was always careful to record my observations into an organized document, which was later to become the Koran. This testament was intended to serve as a confirmation of the Hebrew and Christian Scriptures, and sought only to *perfect* the practices of Judaism and Christianity, not to be perceived as a rebellion against them.

"Once I had observed the "Trinity," as it had been established by the Christians, I could interpret it only as a form of polytheism, which, of course, had been admonished among the Jews, in the Old Testament. I was also aware that the institution of the church was being manipulated so as to offer a paradise of delights to the flesh, which, again, had been forbade in the Bible. I felt that the sincerity of the prayer should best be marked five times daily, throughout the day; and this did not demand that the faithful need seek out the structure of the church.

"As suggested by Mr. Calvin, just a few moments ago, each man carries within him the structure of his personal temple; and so, one need only to face in the direction of Mecca, and bend his knees to the Lord. The prayer is simple, and serves to reaffirm the existence of but the *one* God. Later in the development of the belief, the prayers were formed to cite that I, Mohammed, would be God's Prophet on the Earth.

"There were many things which were found to be lacking in this mundane world, things for which Islam could offer its strength. That which would become of great importance in the scientific community, in the distant future, was the concept of the "zero," a numerical value. There was also a great deal of medical lore handed down, some passing through the land of India, in ways of educating as to the biological structure of the human organism, as well as surgical procedures which could remedy an ailing body.

"However, it was the failing of Christianity which heralded the growth of Islam. The Christian Church had become a harsh feudal lord, taxing the people heavily. The Church made an attempt at domesticating the nomadic Arab tribesman as one of their means for gaining social control. But these people would not accept so drastic a change to their way of life. The Christian Church was itself in a process of change, and a schism had formed between various factions. Those who followed the orthodox church became the persecutors, causing many to turn against it.

"Islam, on the other hand, offered the people a cohesive force, which would be capable of binding believers together in a form of harmony never known before. One must remember that many of these nomadic peoples, scattered throughout the Middle East, and through much of Northern Africa, had never known the concept of unity.

"Sadly, however, Islam began to suffer many of the same ills as had the Christian Church. Originally, Islam had been destined to be headed by the Califa, who would represent the House of Mohammed, offering a guarantee of the purity of the bloodline. However, with time, Caliphs developed out of the families of other than the House of Mohammed, and they would complete for power, which also caused a schism within Islam.

"There evolved a schism between the conservatives and the progressive elements among Islam. Those who believed in the fundamentalism of the Koran were called "Shiites," who were more conservative, and they demanded that their leadership of the Caliphate must follow out of the House of Mohammed.

"On the other hand, the "Sunnites" evolved as the traditionalists, who believed that the Koran must be supplemented by other teachings. In their search for the truth, they held the belief in a Caliphate, which would be headed by some family other than that of Mohammed. As with other great rival factions, these two have been fighting for supremacy since 646 A.D. Between the two, it is the Shiite faction, which is the least tolerant of what they consider "non-believers". Shiite strength is centered in Iraq...but, then again, by this time in Man's history, and with President Bush's assistance, I am sure that all are aware of this last point.

"The coarseness, and the cruelty, of daily life has always been one of those realities, which the average man could, of necessity, learn to tolerate, and even improve upon, through only two means. The first, of course, would be through his *faith*. The other, his *education*, by which I mean the learning of the means by which one may manipulate one's world for the better. And, that belief, which best delivers unto its people these two things, would be that which would gain the greatest exaltation.

"And those religious beliefs which drew men from their lowly condition on Earth, were the same which taught him that cleanliness was "next to Godliness." There were many uncertainties to the average man's life, and one need not fall prey to plague, or illness, as a result of one's own ignorance or filth. The process of Man's seeking that perfection, which was solely the realm of God Himself, could improve Man's lot on Earth.

"While the Islamic follower scheduled his day through the power of the public call to prayer, sung from the minaret, the Christians would accomplish this same effect through the sounding of the church bell, placed in the tower of the church, in each town or village. It may be said that Mankind finally developed its conception of time through this process, carried out by both churches.

The demand of the Christian faith for *blind belief*, or *blind faith*, only served as a hindrance to any progress in the sciences, since it demonstrated little concern for recording data, illuminating change, or developing statistical accuracy. The Medieval Period in Christianity became known as the Age of Faith, for this very reason. All of the mystery of Nature, here spelled with a capital "N," was as yet believed to be of a hidden will, which God alone could determine. Through the "science" of the church, it was predicted that the End-Of-Days, or the Armageddon, would occur in the year 1033 A.D., a date which had been derived from a gathering of materials in the Old Testament. Faced with such dire beliefs, the faith of many in Christianity started to wane, since, with such a brief time remaining for Mankind, each sought the satisfaction of Earthly pleasures before being called to one's eternal reward."

A voice arose from behind. "Certain that the times held little for the common man. The Christians had already modeled their Church estate after the feudal model as their economic reality; and the Church, in Rome, simply became one of those feudal states. Again in Rome, the Pope, also known as the Holy See, became the Defender-Of-The-Faith. At that time, the term was an actual description of his responsibilities, as he became the leader of the Church's feudal army. In the Twenty-First Century, of course, the term Defender-Of-The-Faith is meant as a spiritual defense...but, in Medieval times, the term "defender," was a practical description."

I couldn't quite make out who this was speaking, but, most certainly, he sounded more like an economist than a member of the clergy. Noticing my querulous look, a gentleman next to me added, "We are, after all, discussing that period of Mankind, which was on the verge of the Industrial Revolution. This was a time when there was much reveling in the powers of "Capitalism"."

I was still confused. "And, so; this means...what exactly?"

"It means that there is a great blurring of boundaries between the Church and the State. Up until this point in the history of Man, *land* alone served as the currency of the aristocracy, and the focus of all wealth rested in the soil, in property, and its ownership. Most of that which served man as his victuals, came from the soil, either in the form of vegetation, or as meat from the domesticated animals, which grazed on the land."

"I must be dense, because I'm still having difficulty making this connection between the Church and the manner in which the land was managed," I said.

"The early Church had been ruled by the landed aristocracy, who were the only people with the means, and the leisure, to have been able to take advantage of an education. They carried this principle of the rule of the land, and the economy, into the structure and the function of the Church. You see, it was the Church which had established the "rules of inheritance," citing Bible passages in order to support the continuance of wealth into the next generation. It was also this same Church which served as advocate for the control of lands; and thus, they controlled the wealth of the people. The Church established the codes by which the rules of property ownership could be legitimated, as well as the uses to which they could be placed.

"Along with all of this regulation of ownership, there also developed what would be known as "the sin of acquisition," mainly through Europe, which only served to dilute the purity of religious belief. While the Church was so involved in the acquisition and the use of the lands, the as-yet-unheard voice of *commerce* was in the process of growth. Through this mechanism, one found that there was the concept of *value*, which could now be added to each article, through the process of manufacture and trade; and this was something over which the Church had *not* focused its attention. The artisans and tradesmen were, in fact, mostly those individuals who had been disenfranchised from the ownership of land."

A voice, with a different kind of accent than I had thus far heard, came from behind me. "Oy! Und vat a headache dey made on us!"

When I looked, I noted a gentleman with a long gray beard, gray sideburns, and wearing a yamulka, or skull cap, on his head. Jehovah turned to this man, and said, "Why don't you explain your point, Rabbi?"

"All I had ever heard was how the goyim...sorry...the gentiles questioned why the Jews had become so invested in money. But, believe me; it was not our doing. The Church and the State were considered as one in those days; and it was policy that only landowners could have a vote in the government. This is not so far-fetched, you know. In America, in its early years, it was only the landowners who could vote. But, back to Europe; the law made it clear that Jews could not own real property, or real estate. So, vat vas a man to do? So, the Jews who did come along, settled in the villages, which developed outside the borders of the great estates that were controlled by the land-lords.

"Of course, land alone could never supply the people with all their basic needs for survival, as the soil could not produce "skill" or "crafts." So, many of the Jews became *artisans*, producing the goods which were needed. In time, the artisans in different areas of the countryside had developed a variety of different skills, and each produced commodities which might find favor in another community. As roads sprung up, as routes between the neighboring areas, they offered a path for commerce, a means to trade the produce which had been grown in one place, and make it available in another. With the transport and trade of such produce, the artisans learned that they could transport their wares, as well.

"As the trade routes developed, for the purpose of barter, or the trade of products from one area for those of an other, villages and towns might crop up at certain important intersections, places which could provide services and supplies to these travelers. In time, a *value* was placed on the articles of trade, which increased the raw materials to be worked by the value of the labor which was added to it, and the skill of the workmanship. As a result of this process, a commercial economy was evolving. This was an insidious process, slowly growing, in which the controls of the economy slipped out of the hands of the Church officials, and the aristocrats.

"The Protestant Revolution had focused its energies on the land as the source of all life to Man, as well as the "sweat-equity" put into that soil in order to produce the crops. The Protestant Church would go so far as to discourage trade, through their definition of the *evils* to be found in certain sources of wealth, and making *avarice* the greatest of the sins. However, believing in the practical, one might find that the spoilage of produce stored for later barter might be a greater sin. A quandary had developed. How to stabilize the value of that produce if it was not to be used immediately?

"The response to this fundamentalist quagmire was the development of a system of *currency*, a representational paper, stone, or metal emblem, which would stand for a certain quantity of the actual product. The currency represented the actual product which it could purchase, rather than possessing an abstract value in itself; and it would be easier to carry and trade, with the real product to follow. No longer had one to carry great quantities of produce from place to place, damaging goods, and losing value.

"Since they were not allowed to own any real property, the Jewish villagers were not bound by the rules of trade of the Protestant Church. They were thus coerced into playing the role of the middle-man between the producers of the product, and the purchasers; and, in this way, they became the *currency traders*. In this same way, they were able to convert the currency of any one region into either the currency of another, or directly into the produce the people were seeking."

"It's becoming clearer to me, now," I thought. "Once the economy had converted over to this currency system, the Jewish people found themselves with both the knowledge of this system, and the experience of trading in currency. Am I right?"

"Smart, Boychick! You got a cupella on your shoulders. As the economy was changing, the focus of capitalism soon settled in Holland and England. Why, you ask?...OK, I'll tell you. Both of these nations are nearly surrounded by water, the ocean; and they depend, to a large extent, on these waterways for getting their necessities for life. Also, these nations supported worldwide exploration, which helped to uncover new products, and new sources of wealth, which they then brought back to the European continent. From this exploration, we discovered chocolate from Mexico, vanilla beans from the Pacific, and new sources of sugar, which actually became worth its weight in gold in Europe.

"So, the Jews had...if you'll excuse the analogy...a *nose* for money. The Jew would prosper from the field of trade, into which he had been forced by the laws of the Church. And then, he was ostracized for his skills, as if it were something he had stolen from the Church.

'Oy, vay! Ven vill dey effer learn?!!'"

"Mr. Smith? Would you please offer your own observations on the developments which followed?" asked Jehovah.

"Who?" I asked.

"Oh, that's Adam Smith, the economist. He wrote a lot about the changes in the world as a result of the rise of capitalism. Between he, and that guy, Machiavelli, one can gain quite an understanding of what is meant by the term, power politics."

"I thank you , Sir. I would love to offer my own views on the subject.

"To this point in history, political thought centered on the ownership of real property, evolving into a predominantly agrarian economy. With this expansion of trade, and the birth of the Industrial Revolution, one could witness a *secularization* of political thought, especially in Europe. Politics developed into a "science," which followed certain established rules and laws for varying procedures, and would no longer be simply a matter of philosophical debate.

"As you may remember, to this point, the sole seat of wisdom and education had rested in the Church, and was in the command of those who owned the land. The institutionalization of religion had followed a similar growth pattern. It soon became perceived as vulgar, or common, for one to soil one's hands by working in the earth. Thus, even the landed gentry became the personification of vulgarity, poorly educated, and relying on clerics, who they would invite to reside on their manors for the communication skills which they found necessary in order to reach beyond the walls of their manor. For those who may be interested in examining this situation, one need only view the movie, <u>Tom Jones</u>, which presented all of this material so clearly, down to the local clergy invited in to educate the youth. The clergy might offer such education as was necessary to teach the most basic skills to the descendents of the lord of the manor.

"The study of the sciences also rested within the walls of the Church; but the content of that scientific field was also to be controlled by the Church, and was directed by Church doctrine. It was the Church which had command over the rules for social morality, and which determined that which was accepted as proper behavior. *However*, the one area of human endeavor, which appears to have slipped through the fingers of the organization of the Church, was *economics*.

"If one is to understand, and accept, this concept, then it would be possible to better comprehend the fact that economic affaires were *not* governed by the "rules of good conscience," the power of which still rested within the Church. The Church, and its control over social morality, demanded a certain degree of conservatism, perceiving this as the path to the greater good for Mankind. However, in the field of economics, many concessions would be made in the name of individualism. The *letter of the law* was not exactly the same things as the concept of *moral rule*.

"From this line of thinking, there evolved the concept that man is a product of his environment. Religion had sought to teach the rule of "predestination," which states that one's future lay solely within the hands of God. Thus, a chasm had developed between these two philosophical schools of religion and economics.

"If one were to attempt an outline of the ideal society, one might observe a particular community, which might be made up of unequal classes, but each such class serving some integral function in the process of the whole. Altogether, they would be directed toward a common end.

"If this community is to be an ideal economic community, one might find that it operates on the basis of a *self-adjusting mechanism*. This would be a situation in which the functioning of society would be based on the interplay of economic motives, aiming at supplying the economic needs of the community. And, it may be here that a conflict would develop, between the economic ideals, and the religious ideals.

"Thinking *ethically*, an individual should not take advantage of his neighbor, whether by manipulation of economic necessities, or by the taking advantage of weaknesses in function. In *economic* terms, however, man's self-love is God's providence. In the religious community, one's religious standards may be adequate to suppress the individual's economic appetites; while, in economic terms, expediency may become the major criterion for a choice of possible actions.

"The type of thinking, which I have just suggested, may appear perplexing to those who have witnessed the political scene in America recently. The Republican Party has long expressed its favor for an economic style in which the power of the market holds sway. It preaches that government must not interfere in the natural play of economic forces. However, in terms of economic theory, morality, if expressed on a limited scope, would represent the wolf devouring the lamb, so to speak. Those who are best able to supply the public's needs will eventually command the market, no matter how many smaller vendors may be "devoured" in the process. And then, by this same law of economic reality, once that force has taken control of the market, it would be unimpeded from carrying out ventures which would be in its own favor, without respect to the general welfare of that society.

"I am on record as believing that there is often a confusion due to this line of thinking; and it emerges within the apparent conflict which exists between those of the "far right," and those of the "left." Those of the far right preach a devout form of religion and moral conscience while, at the same time, they preach a laissez-faire economic policy. What this suggests is that, if one were to leave the economic market to its own influences, it would naturally seek "balance," which the theory conceives of as favorable to the consumer, issuing the lowest possible price. This is *not*, in point of fact, what actually happens. Even if those with conservative political beliefs were to seek moderation, they are, after all, still just humans. Given any advantage in this economic market, the individual will tend to *bleed* the market for profits, if for no other reason that *it can*.

"If there were a large market to open in a particular area, and its buying power allowed it to sell to the consumer at a price which would be much lower than any smaller competitor, it would most likely drive the other stores out of the market. However, once the competition ceases to function effectively, the larger store would feel free to charge whatever level the market would then bare. Isn't this, after all, what the Twentieth and Twenty-First Centuries have found true of petroleum production? Without a viable competitor, those in the petroleum business can get whatever they want for their product."

I had to admit that the man made sense. If I had the only game in town, and I knew that the people wanted to play, I would certainly be holding the strings on this puppet show. It was becoming obvious that there were many things which influence philosophy, I mean beyond the mere cognitive exercise of pulsing blood through the frontal lobes. Not all that purports to be humanitarian is in fact for the general good of Man. Morality and ethics were pretty hairy concepts once one enters the field of economics.

Adams Smith continued. "By the time that the Protestant Revolution had arrived in Europe, the organized Church had itself become a very dominant political institution, having, by that time, learned well from the economic sector. It was obvious that this change had been a necessary one, since the Church had realized that it could no longer maintain its traditional control over its followers simply through the doctrines which it had preached. But, its excesses were suffocating its own efforts, and it was becoming susceptible to the same lay principles as did politics and economics. The Sixteenth Century has been cited as a transition point for both religious and economic thought.

"The paths of religious thought then followed the strongest trade routes, which ran predominantly from East to West, and from North to South. Soon, there developed an active trade in *ideas*, as well as in goods. The widest change appears to have occurred in those areas in which the travel for trade were to start, as well as those locations at which they were to intersect. And here, I beseech Mr. Charles Darwin to offer his explanation, to clarify the developments in human evolution.

"If you please, Dr. Darwin."

"I thank you, Sir.

"I am not sure how many within this group are familiar with my stories on the evolution of living things; and I encourage those of you with divergent views to attempt some measure of deference to these ideas that I present. I am reminded of the Snopes incident, again, as mentioned earlier, which begs me to hesitate before discussing my views. I do not wish to be perceived as a heretic."

Jehovah presumed to speak for all, when he stated, "Please carry on, Sir. I'm sure we are all interested to hear what you have to say."

"It has long been my belief that there exists a general flow within Nature, as there is within the field of physics. By those same laws of physics, we are aware that energy will flow in the path of least resistance, such as the flow of liquid following a downhill path rather than attempting to climb any heights unassisted. It would seem, then, that Man's social and mental forces would follow a similar path, and grow from a baser form, in the direction of greater complexity, in order that it might meet the needs of the individual organism. Society, as a whole, is made up of individuals, or separate organisms, each of which may be conceived of as differing in some way, whether it be physical, cognitive, or psychological. The *Law of Natural Selection* will favor those organisms which possess the greatest ability to prosper, to adapt, as well as to benefit Mankind in general. In so doing, there would develop a natural *hierarchy*, in which the strongest organisms would lead.

"Within each such level of this hierarchy, there would be a balance established, with each of the members providing the necessary services to the whole, in proportion to each one's ability. The importance which develops from this, is whether or not there is any form of *governance* of this communal effort, that it all serve a common goal in the end, something which may be shared by all the members of that society.

"We may thus describe this as the *physics of human organization*, and note that it, too, follows some of those same scientific laws of physics. And, perhaps, this could be the reason that one might describe the study of politics as a "science," since it does follow certain established laws.

"Society, as a whole, may be conceived of as, itself, a living organism unto itself. It is composed of a head, and it possesses different parts, all of which function relatively independently, and each possessing its own identifiable functions. Each part serves its own integrated function in the entirety of the grand scheme of things; and each part, within any particular level of functioning, may be perceived as being equal.

"Society appears to be held together by a system of mutual, though varying, obligations. Within the Church, one may perceive the organization, as a whole, to be serving God, each in its own way. Though there be numerous, and differing, religious beliefs, and different ways in which one may define one's philosophy, each may be equal, and each may serve God in its own way.

"But, since we are here dealing with the human organism, which, after all, is quite complex, we are dealing with an organism which perceives itself as possessing the power of *self-determination*. In the process of evolution, there appears to have developed a competition between some of the varying parts of the whole, each challenging the "union," while possessing a perception of its own aims and purposes. Each has created a specific goal, which it then seeks to protect. In the industrial arena, this process has been carried out by the formation of guilds, and then unions, each expressing its own vested interests.

"In those arenas, in which one finds *avarice*, there then occurs a deterioration of social organization. Our learned associate has described this process earlier in our discussion, in terms of the Church, which was then centered in Rome. Power and prestige became salable commodities, and ideals, in the abstract or ethereal, seemed to fade. The Papacy of the Middle Ages, in fact, became the greatest financial institution on Earth, and its coffers still hold one of the world's largest accumulations of wealth. While that church continues to preach "the common good," it also focuses on one's attaining of one's reward for a life well lived, but only a reward received in Heaven. And so, what is it that one is to do with the Earthly wealth it has accumulated, if not to assist the general existence of Mankind?

"It is indeed a perplexing dilemma which we face, when we examine the ideals which are set forth through religious doctrine, and then we compare it to the practices of that institution of the Church, which may be ruled through the human frailties!"

Hmmmmmmmmmm! That's a lot to digest in such a short time. And, it is certainly complicated. At what point, exactly, does the "Word of God" end, and the "thinking of Man" begin?

Jehovah was correct, all right. Maybe He just hadn't written this one down quite clearly enough for Man to follow. I don't think that He could send enough representatives to the Earth in any effort at achieving an adequate level of understanding.

As I looked around, I found that I was not alone in my thinking; everyone else seemed to be scratching their heads, as well. They sat quietly, staring into the fire, long into the night, until sleep overcame them. But, from the rustling around me, I could tell that, even in their sleep, they continued to wrestle with the confusion which had been uncovered.

Chapter Ten

I found that I had tossed and turned throughout the night, as if I had been trying to make some sense from all that I had heard. So much was what I had already believed; but there was much to be digested, and which jostled my thoughts. Curiously enough, however, finding myself in this wilderness, among these representatives of the world's religious and philosophical schools, was not even a consideration at this point. You would have thought that this kind of experience would be enough for me to buy that ticket to the booby-hatch; especially *me*, the small-town shrink that I am.

Maybe it was the fact that *nothing* that had thus far occurred in the past few days was very far from what I had already dared to think of, myself, at some time or other in my life. I guess that this is something which might be true for almost any human being, no matter how committed that person may be to any particular system of beliefs.

Gee, I wonder if God, Himself, ever held any doubts!

I mean, well, let's take the case of a chef, for example. Even the greatest chef in the world may sometimes question one of his own creations. Even though he will taste it as he is preparing the dish, isn't it also true that he may hover just above his guests, as they place their forks into that creation, and bring that first taste to their lips? We *all* want to be certain that we've done all that we could do to make the very best of our efforts.

And, that just leads to another question in my mind...If Man **is**, in fact, created in the image of God, as we are sometimes told, would it then be true to say that our *flaws* also come from Him? I mean, if He is **perfect**, then that which He creates would have to be exactly what He intended it to be...Right?!

But, if He intended these flaws to exist in Man's character, then how could He expect any individual to reach that level of existence which would have earned him that entrance into Heaven?

If one chooses to examine this question, in this manner, one might do better to consider the deities of Mankind evolving out of the Greek and Roman culture, living atop Mount Olympus, in the Earthly capital, competing with each other over the course which Mankind might take...Kinda like a giant chess game.

Could *that* possibly be what the God of the Jews, the God of the Christians, and the God of the Moslems would do? Did He *purposely* create these imperfections, perhaps just to see if His creation could seek to better itself? Perhaps this would be like picking a cat up, and then dropping it upside-down, just to watch if it will land on its feet.

But, He must have created those flaws; after all, He is *omnipotent*, isn't He? He is all things, and He is all-powerful. He gives life, and He takes it away.

Or, maybe it would be better to seek out a video rental store, and just view <u>Oh, God</u>!, again. Somehow, for me at least, I find it a comforting image...I mean, George Burns, in those squeaky sneakers, puffing on a cigar, representing the God of all Mankind. In that movie, God is presented as **One** who has had a hand in creating that which is. The power of self-direction was left to each creation, to seek its own path through this life.

Would that be in conflict with all that has been thus far described here? There are those who have stated that they believed the world is *absolute*, and that it has been created *exactly* as God would have it. According to this belief system, it is Man's job to search out that meaning to life, in order to set out upon the path which the Maker has set for us.

On the other hand, there are those who believe that Man's position in this world is one of greater liberation from all these controlling forces. For them, it is *the world* which holds the potential of perfection. Thus, Man's job is to seek that perfection in the world.

"I am what I am!"...That's what God had said.

What do you think *that* means?

If *I* had made a grammatical statement like that, when I was in school, I bet that I'd have been assigned an extra homework assignment, you know? Of course, it has also been said that no man can ever fully *know* God, since it is only God who can do *that*. Just *how much* knowledge are we to be allowed to have, then?

The Faust character, in legend, and throughout all of his historical rebirths, has displayed the temerity of believing that he could gain the power to outwit the Devil, through the process of knowing those secrets which have alluded Mankind since the beginnings of time. Does the seeking of endless knowledge mean that one seeks to emulate or, worse, replace, God? What would that say for all those institutions of higher education around the world?

Hmmmmmmm...Did I say *institutions*!

Exactly *what* are we talking about here; one hears the word "institution" being used to cover any number of things. Webster defines the word as a noun, an organization, which has been designed with a specific direction and *purpose.*

Now, isn't that where most of our difficulty arises?

I really haven't heard, or seen, much which could suggest that there are any irresolute differences among any of the world's theological powers...that is, until humans somehow seek to organize that belief system into some form of formal group, with which to translate the Word of God, or to direct Man's efforts, here on Earth. *That's* when we find those little things, like "holy wars," or maybe the "Inquisition," and the like. There have always been men who have used religion as their passport to power. As I've already mentioned, the original Popes, in Rome, were actually generals of the Church, the defenders of the faith.

And, who can ever forget those wonderful Crusades! Or, maybe, the brotherhood of Northern Ireland, or Yugoslavia, or Pakistan and India, or Tibet, or anywhere in the Middle East?

Need I go on? There's been an awful lot done, in the name of God, and in the name of religion, in general. There's also those battles over power, and money, and pride...

Wait a minute!

Aren't all of those things actually supposed to be condemned by the major religions, somewhere along the way! Well, pride, for sure. I seem to remember John Calvin talking recently; and, according to him, strict Protestantism looks down on the seeking after power over one's fellow man, or the greed of seeking after wealth, especially when done in an effort at subjugating one's fellow man.

I had been lost in my own head there for a while. As I looked around, I noticed that others were beginning to stir. So, I reached my arm out, to stir the embers of the fire, in an effort at being able to heat the water for our morning beverage. Mog was already astir. He could be heard beating the brush around his cave entrance. Whenever this occurred, it was a certain message to the others, around him, to get themselves up and ready to face the day...Or, at least, to be capable of ducking Mog's club.

There was a definite chill in the air this morning, and so, everyone gathered a little closer to the fire, rubbing their hands and feet, and trying to get the circulation moving. Across the fire from where I sat, I noticed a cute young woman, little more than an adolescent; but she was dressed in chainmail. She stood in place, and beckoned the others to join her in some morning calisthenics.

"Who's that?"

Moses smiled. "Jean D'Arc...Uh, Joan of Arc...She treats every morning as if it were her own personal campaign of some sort..." He turned to her, and shouted, "Hey! Joan! Sit down; we'll do something *after* we've had some breakfast, and gotten this chill off."

He turns back to me, and says, "I'll tell you something; the last *real* exercise I got was when I climbed that darn mountain, way back there, after we'd finally left Egypt. I just had to get away from those crybabies, all seeking something to believe in...something they could actually *see*...You know what I mean?"

"You talking about Mount Sinai, where you received the Ten Commandments from God?"

"Thirteen, actually."

"Thirteen? What do you mean?"

161

"There were originally thirteen commandments. But, after we talked about it for a while, we realized that thirteen seemed to be such an *unlucky* number. So, we pared it down, little by little, trying to figure out how many we could ask the people to sacrifice, you know, before they'd feel that we were really pushing.

"Ten sounded like a good, round number. It contained all the basics, you know...don't kill, don't steal, don't slut around, seek out a little structure and dignity in your family...that kind of stuff."

"Pretty *profound*, I'd say."

Moses put his hand to his chin, looked into the distance, smiled, and then turned back to me. "You know something, that was probably the first *prescription* for happiness!"

"How do you mean?"

"Well, you know the doctor's old adage, don't you; Take two tablets, and call me in the morning!"

Jeers could be heard all around. It was still a little too early in the morning for this. Someone yelled out, "Enough already. The world isn't ready for the *First Church of Burlesque!*"

So, we all sat back, and enjoyed a small repast, before our morning aerobics, ala Joan.

The meals were always pretty intriguing. Let's see, how could I best describe them? There was never a simple menu, with something simple, like eggs, or pancakes, or oatmeal. But, then again, what exactly had I expected those gathered here to eat? One has, of course, heard of the ambrosia of the gods, for example.

Then again, one might think that the *deities* might have no need of *nutrition*; but that would be a consideration for only those of an ethereal, rather than mortal, birth. Remember, many theological and philosophical belief systems have been based on leaders who had, at one time, been of mortal birth, and who had achieved deification through the process of self-perfection on the human playing field. Having once been human, they would have had to have partaken of these nutrients for their survival. So, I guess that food would have to be a conceivable part of their everlasting existence.

Furthermore, while we are talking about those who had been able to survive the tribulations of their humanity, we may have to consider all that they may have experienced, such as a variety of, shall we say, *other appetites*...huh?!!

Mankind has always been led to believe that the appetites of Man only show up his frailties; a "true god" would have no *need* for anything other than himself, or herself. Wouldn't a god-figure be fully self-fulfilled, and complete?

I must have been thinking out loud for, as these thoughts passed through my consciousness, a few of the figures around me had started to discuss this issue aloud. Jehovah tapped me on the shoulder, and said, "Don't you remember that little admission I made about my penmanship? I can't blame others for too many things, not with a penmanship as bad as mine can be.

"I don't know...the Greeks may have had it right, after all...Perfection may simply be an ideal, one which may exist in the mind alone. But, that doesn't have to mean that one should cease to seek after that perfection! The path leading through existence can be fraught with all sorts of obstacles.

"I seem to remember that you had expressed some thoughts about life, looking at it on all levels, as being similar in structure to that of the atom. It may have been your flaw to conceive of that atom as a "universe," when it may have actually been more readily defined as a "solar system." Atoms join to form molecules, molecules join to create matter, matter joins to create the known material world, and the planets then find their balance around their own particular solar sources, or their "suns." All that is known, when everything is considered together, has been defined as a "universe."

"With so many dynamic interacting spheres of organic and inorganic mass, one must always expect that there will be some form of imperfection; that's simply inescapable. Each action may be calculated as precisely as possible, but that may only be appropriate for that exact moment in time. Conditions are always in a state of flux, or change, moment to moment. Much of what occurs in the universe may be ascribed to the workings of "circumstance." While each of the elements in any interaction may be under one's control, there is usually *some* resultant condition, which cannot be perfectly, or fully, predicted.

"Isn't this, after all, the major premise of scientific thought? A test situation may be arranged, in which one is attempting to control every factor which is possible. The real test is when one examines the outcome of our operation. One manipulates all of the factors one can, in order that one may study the effects on those elements which have not been so controlled, or which may have been unknown."

"So, what, exactly, is *real*, and what *isn't*? What, then, am I supposed to *trust*? Am I to trust my senses, or must I relinquish all belief to the power of the deities, and trust *them* to properly direct my life?"

Jehovah sat back. "Whoa! Hey, wait a minute, there!"

"Why?"

"Nobody's been asked to relinquish *anything*!

"To demand that humanity blindly obey the commands of the deities would place an awful lot of responsibility on *us*!

For *that* to be possible, would demand that there be a constant process of communication between Mankind and his chosen god, or gods. To read, or hear, the laws which have been set forth for Mankind to follow, would be insufficient to insure that these laws would be carried out. You've already seen what happened with that experiment with Moses...You know, the Ten Commandments? No sooner had Moses, here, gotten back from his little sojourn to the mountain, than he found his people dancing the jig around one of the jeweler's Saturday Night Specials. It's just not possible, even for *us*, to be that invested.

"Have you ever taken care of an infant? You gotta be on your toes, Kiddo, I'll tell you! All you gotta do is make one indiscreet comment, unthinkingly, and you'll hear it echoed from the kid. If you want to teach something to people, you have to be willing to put in the time to systematically reinforce that which you are trying to teach; and you must make certain that they understand *precisely* what you're trying to convey."

"This is certainly getting complicated...So, how does one *teach* Mankind the proper path in life?"

Again, Jehovah chuckled at my naivete. "Proper, smopper! What's proper is related to the particular individual, to that particular time in his life, to those particular sets of circumstances, and to a multiplicity of factors which are difficult, if at all possible, to control."

"So, what you're saying is that life is a haphazard roller-coaster ride, which one climbs onto a birth, and just rises and falls throughout life, until he or she reaches that big finish?"

"No!! It's better planned than *that*! As for myself, I've managed to put in some extra effort in the evolution of some special resources for Man to learn from. You remember that stuff about the Garden of Eden? Well, there was this piece of property, between these two rivers, in what is now the Middle

East; a place which could be compared to places like, say, Miami, Honolulu, or, maybe, Fiji, all wrapped up into one. Such a place...Oy! When I was considering what it might be to fulfill that "Big Picture," I thought to myself...Self, where in this world would you find it the easiest to get a fair start on life? Where could one have the greatest chance of succeeding in developing something, called *Humanity*? And this is what I came up with."

"So, what happened? It didn't all go the way you planned it, did it?"

"You gonna fault me for *that*, huh? Look, it was the *perfect* setting. I figured, what could screw this up? But, remember, Adam and Eve were only the prototypes, the originals. *Every* new creation has a few kinks to work out. All of them need some kind of "fine-tuning," in order that they will eventually work properly. I knew, right away, when that serpent refused to shake hands on the deal, that things were headed into the crapper.

"Of the many born to Man, we, the deities that is, made certain to personally involve ourselves in the creation of a few individuals whom we believed would truly earn our trust; that were of such stature and virtue that we felt they might best pass on The Word...the way we meant it to be taught, that is. Most of the deities had made allowances in The Plan for humans to exercise the power of *self-determination*. While there would always be a path, which was designed to lead to the ultimate reward, the exact course which one could take was always a matter of choices. Why? Well, without choices, all we would have would be a group of puppets, and it would have to be up to *us* to pull all of the strings.

"It is also of importance to keep in mind that *that* which was created, was placed here for the satisfaction of the *deities*.

Whether one considers it to be a flaw or not, much of Mankind holds a conception of the deities as *anthropomorphic* representations; that is to say, they have been conceived as possessing the form, the thinking, the needs, and the actions of humans. Diversity was another element of the great plan, from the beginning. It was diversity that provided Man with a sense of creativity. For the gods, as for man, boredom may be the only consequence of continuous "sameness". If all things were endlessly predictable, the same, and unchanging, there might be little, if any, motivation to action. Again, I refer to that earlier discussion, the one about the solar system, and how any unit of matter, or energy, which may be thrown out of balance, may force the entire system to seek a new equilibrium."

I guess that would be what one calls a *truism*, that any life, which is acted out in pure *rote*, or mechanically, could very well lack the power to enervate either thought or *action*. "Please, I gotta know. What is the truer reality for Man; what we *sense*, or what we *think*?"

"Are you sure that you want an answer to this one? I can tell you, it drove Renee Descartes a little nuts, just in his effort at coming to terms with a logical proof of existence. He gathered all his *cognitive* skills, his knowledge of mathematics, and he applied this scientific methodology to the problem of human existence.

"The result...COGITO ERGO SUM...I think, therefore, I am...!

"But, that doesn't totally answer your question, does it?

"Let's see; we've quoted the Greeks, whose belief it was that perfection is an ideal, which is held in the mind as a purity of thought, and that all that is left to Man on this Earth would be to seek after that perfection. In the process of that search, Man's tools for that search would have to be his *senses*. However, we've also suggested that action and behavior tend to be the victim of circumstance, no matter how well it is that we plan our actions.

"I think that what Descartes was trying to say with his mathematical proof was that thought and action are one, in the end. Have you ever awakened from a dream, and still had that feeling that you may still be in that process of whatever your dream depicted you as doing?"

"Yeh, why sure."

"So, you tell me; What was the reality? Was it, perhaps, the thought alone? Or was it the feeling that your body was expressing in the action, as you were again trying to regain consciousness?"

"I don't really know that it's *possible* to separate the two; is it?"

"You got it, Kiddo! Your nervous system is involved in both processes, of thinking, and of sensing. Which comes first? In the end, is it really that important a distinction? Without the ability to think, the sensations would not mean anything. Without the ability to sense, thinking would simply be stagnant and unchanging.

"Each human possesses a differing ability with regard to these two processes. It is as important for those who can think productively, and organize all knowledge of Man, as it is for those with the physical prowess to enact those plans. All that stuff, about demeaning those who possess lesser cognitive skills, is only an attempt to deny their value as humans. Each creation possesses potential, and each possesses a *value* simply by the fact of his existence. After all, if you happen to have a pound of gold hidden in a drawer, isn't it worth just as much as a pound of gold which has been coined as currency? They can each be perceived as being an expression of the same thing; it is only the manner in which they are used which varies."

Hmmmmmmmmm...I think, and therefore, I am, huh? Mind and body *do* work most effectively when they function together, in *unity.*"

While the rest of the deities nodded their heads in agreement, Jehovah said, "Of even greater significance, then, especially for humans, might be the statement that **I THINK, THEREFORE, <u>YOU</u> ARE!**"

"What do you mean by *that*?"

"It is Man's ability to think that enables him to embody a spirit, much like that of the deities. Of course, *you* can see, hear, and touch us...and, in at least one case here," he said, as he looked to the far end of the gathering, toward the cave, "even *smell* us...while, for the majority of humanity, the deities remain intangible; they remain a *belief*...a *hope.* The very fact that humans are capable of *creating* images in their minds, enables the deities to exist in a cooperative relationship with Man."

It seemed that each clarification just brought another question to my mind; but I had to ask. "You, know, I've been here for a while now; and I've become accustomed to your presence, I mean the form in which you present yourselves to me...or, am I to more properly state it as *"Yourself"*? Whatever...I haven't really given it much thought, at least not until *this* moment...but, you know how it has become a favorite belief of Mankind that man is created in God's image? As I am looking around me, at most of you *here*, I can see variations in size, in costume, and in custom; but you really all appear to be quite "human," if that's the right term to use!"

I noticed the deities all looking at each other, mulling over what I had asked. They all seemed to look to Jehovah, who was serving as the spokesman, I guess. Jehovah was pondering the question, too; he crossed his arms at his chest, raised one hand to his face, and stroked his beard. After He looked off into the distance for a moment, and then looked directly into my eyes. "Exactly *how* would you see me, I mean, if you were to have the choice?"

"What do you mean? You're starting to sound more and more like Dr. Freud...answering a question with a question."

"What is the image of God that you would actually *wish* to see? Mankind has created an image of the many characters which he could possibly see, such as Santa Claus, the Tooth Fairy, Father Time...It seems important for Mankind to find an image, which enables him to function more effectively in the world."

"Are you saying that there is no *one*, indisputable image by which you are known?"

"That reminds me of a joke..." This led to some grumbling from those gathered around us. I could hear someone say, "Uh-oh, here we go again!" And then there was some chuckling.

Unflinchingly, Jehovah continued. "I remember this joke, which was going around in America, back during the Civil Rights demonstrations in the South, and when people were expressing their "Black Power" for all to see. Well, it seems that this man went under the knife, for open-heart surgery; and, for just a moment during the operation, his heart stopped, and his soul left his body. The doctor told everyone to keep this under their hats, since neither the patient, nor his family, seemed emotionally strong enough to handle the situation.

"The surgical team was able to revive the man, and to successfully complete the surgery. It appeared that the patient had made a full recovery, and was about to be discharged from the hospital, when the surgeon conducted his final examination, just to make certain that everything was still functioning as it should. Feeling that the man was strong enough by this time, the surgeon decided to tell him what had taken place in the operating room, expecting an expression of gratitude for his revival, and the return to his family.

"However, rather than appearing surprised by this news, he simply stated, "Yeh, I know." It was too much for the doctor to deal with, and he just asked, "Just *how* did you know *that*?" The man answered, "Oh! Because I went to Heaven." Suspecting that this brief lapse in the surgery may have resulted in some unforeseen psychiatric reaction, the doctor responded, "Heaven? Mmmmmmm...Just how do you know *this*?" The patient answered, "Because I met God, and I was told that it just wasn't *my* time, yet; and that I would be sent back to my family."

"The doctor was incredulous. "You say you met *God*? What was God like?"

"The patient just looked up at the doctor, and quietly said, *"She's Black!"*

"So, you see, I guess that any deity is only what each man is capable of seeing and accepting at any particular moment in his life. I'm afraid that Mankind does not possess a limitless amount of tolerance, and seems to have established a firm set of standards within which he will deal with things.

"That guy...Who was that?...Oh, yeh; Rod Sterling...From that TV show, The Twilight Zone...and, maybe, some of those episodes from Star Trek...whenever some supernatural event presents itself to the hero...well, in many of the cases, the entity would say that it would take on that form which the person would best tolerate, since it was not felt that Mankind was prepared for their *real* image."

"Gee!" I thought. "I'd always considered myself to be something of a Renaissance Thinker, a man of the world; so, I never believed that Man would place these kinds of limitations on himself. But, do *you* think so little of Mankind; I mean, to believe that he actually has such limitations?"

"Have you ever tried any of that new "green" ketchup on your fries?"

"Yeccccchhh! OK; point taken."

"It will, most likely, always be an issue, that each man must feel comfortable with the presence of his deity, if he is to be able to listen, and to respond, to that deity. That which the individual believes, will ever become a part of him. I guess that's what they're talking about when they say that God made man in His own image. It would probably be more accurate to present the reverse of that statement, and to say that it is Mankind which creates its deities in the image of Man.

"Even in the movies, when an individual is presented talking aloud, in the presence of no other visible individual, and he is not speaking into any kind of mechanism, he is looked upon as being "sick in the head." If one could imagine another person, standing at that person's side, throughout the conversation, then the situation may prove to be more acceptable. When people pray, whether it be in church, or in the home, I believe that they probably interject that image of their deity which presents itself in human form. That would make the process of communication more rational...maybe, even acceptable."

It had been a long day, and there was a lot to mull over. I decided to ask a favor of Mog, and I asked if I might borrow his cave for awhile. I took a seat at the fire, and just stared into the flames, watching them dance and spit. With the warmth of the fire on my face and my body, combined with the rhythmic movements of the flames, I soon found myself in a sort of trance, lost in my own reveries.

Chapter Eleven

I was roused from my somewhat hypnotic state by the hub-bub, both at the campfire around me, and from outside the cave itself. It would seem that the previous discussion had most definitely fired some heavy discussion within the congregation, and between the various factions represented. I had to poke my head out, and see what was cooking.

I stepped out from the cave, still stretching, and trying to squeeze the last of the sedentary lactic acid from my muscles, and clear the cobwebs from my eyes.

I soon realized that it was, in fact, *I*, who was the center of the controversy. I guess I hadn't considered that *my* presence could have as profound an effect on these characters as they had had no me. For myself, it was easy to identify these figures as "deities," just that they were "in-the-flesh" representations of the entities with which I was already familiar, through my studies at least. Each had always been capable of functioning effectively in their form, whatever that customarily was, or as each had been presented for centuries on Earth. They had never had the situation presented to them in which they would be made to confront themselves, or to question whether there was, in fact, some *absolute* identify into which each was to settle.

Not until *I* came on the scene, and started raising questions which they may never have had to deal with. Perhaps they were feeling the need to reaffirm their own identities, as well as their purpose in the scheme of the universe. I guess that makes them much like humans, who habitually perform their regular and expected tasks throughout life, without questioning their role. One doesn't become fully aware of what one is doing until some focus is placed upon oneself.

Maybe it was time for me to pose the **Big Question**!

What the heck; we've gotten this far. What did I have to lose by jumping in with both feet?

"Who...or What...is God?...There, I said it!"

It was as if a great vacuum tube had burst, as I could hear a gasp from each of those present. And then, there was a profound silence for several minutes. Had I finally overstepped my bounds? Had I, indeed, gone too far, this time?

I took a quick survey of conditions...The ground wasn't rumbling beneath me, there was no great bursts of thunder and lightning...Just that silence!

I couldn't stand it any more; I had to break this silence before it would eat me alive. "There's just been so much in the way of diversity and differences in the way that each of you have presented your own personal experience of Mankind, from that most "primitive" Earth-Mother, to the most philosophical proofs of existence, as offered by Monsieur Descartes.

"I had made note that some of those presented as deities, had presented themselves as being humans, who had somehow managed to raise themselves above the emptiness of humanity...And there were those, who had been unable to place any date on their births, nor could they perceive any potential for an end to their existence. Is the faith, of which you all speak, to be conceived of as a "real" power, here on Earth; or is it to be considered as an abstract entity, which we may use as our guide along our path, here on Earth?"

Everyone seemed to be responding to this question, each in his own tongue; but *I* could hear a singular voice over all the others.

"The Buddha, which is the eventual name by which he has been known, would serve best as an example of that idealized state to which all men should seek. It was said that he had been born of Man, but has *earned* his deification, not only through his acts, here on the Earth, but also through the sincerity and earnestness of his beliefs.

"It is possible for one to conceive of perfection as the absolute embodiment of some particular quality, a condition which one might not expect amidst all the imperfection that is found in the tangible universe. It is an *abstract*. It is *theoretical*.

"Thus, if Mankind is to somehow attain this state of perfection, one might say that this man is seeking to become one with an "abstract." Furthermore, it could be stated that the very concept of a God is, itself, an "abstract". Was it not one of the Greek philosophers who stated that all which exists in this world is nothing more, or less, than an imperfect reflection of some *ideal*, which can exist in the pureness of thought, alone?

"As humanity has evolved from one evolutionary stage to another, we find that there has been an associated evolution in his cognitive and philosophical capacities, as well. In his primitive form, Mankind functioned as did any human infant. As such, he could experience only the *now*, only *here*; so that all that existed in the infant's world would be those things which are able to exist only as far as his *senses* allow him to experience.

"As that infant matures, however, his nervous system begins to establish a set of networks, each designed to deal with all of the new data entering from outside of the organism; and it combines with all that the infant already learned about the *inside* of his body. Cognitive skills develop, and these allow the child to pass beyond a state of pure sensation, and to eventually delve into one's projections of *alternative realities*, which we might define as "*imagination.*" In terms of Mankind, as a whole, this process probably developed with the evolution of the Cro-Magnon.

"With this evolution of Man, into the arena of abstract thought, it now became possible for each man to carry, within him, his own god or gods. It was no longer necessary that a god be *concretely* represented in some positive form, perhaps as a drawing on the wall of a cave, and representing the beasts which he planned to hunt. Man's deities became "portable," and more flexible...and, one might say, even more of a *personalized* god, which satisfied the needs and desires of that particular individual. While it is possible that several people might gather, and all, together, offer some common prayer to their deity, there is no way of being able to see that each was actually dealing with that very same image of that deity."

"Is that such a terrible thing?" I asked. "I mean, one need only look at all the crap going on in the Middle East, or in Ireland, or in Afghanistan! Why does Man demand that his fellow man accept only *that* image of God as the *only* image? *SHOULD* every man be forced to accept a singular concept of God?"

"I can remember Anthony Newly attempting to offer an answer to that one, in his play, Stop the World, I Want to Get Off. The answer was placed in the song, "What Kind of Fool Am I?" Do you really think that *that* is what I'm all about....Making every man exactly the same! How gauche! I don't want to blow my own horn, but I'm better than *that*!

"Look, if I'm really seeking toward some form of "creativity" in Man, I have to be able to set some kind of example for him. It would be the same for any form of parenting; one teaches best when one teaches by example. That's why it's so important to be careful of what one says or does in the presence of the young...because it may come back to bite you in the ass!"

"You've been touted as being the "Almighty," the "omnipotent," the "omnipresent." If it's truly up to each man to create his own image of God for himself, then just what are You, that I can try to form some conception in my mind, around which I might develop my concept of God?"

I thought to myself, "Maybe NOW I'll get a straight and direct answer." Finally, the question was out there.

There was an anxious hesitation that seemed to last for an extremely long time. And then, in an incredibly booming voice, came the answer.

"I am <u>everything</u>...I am <u>nothing</u>...Just remember that <u>I</u> <u>am</u>!"

"Is that it?!!! You're not going to let me off with this easily, are you? You're going to make me work for it!" Hmmmmm...Maybe, *that's* it; maybe it's something we must *each* answer for ourselves!

"I am the <u>One</u>...I am the <u>Singular</u>...I am the <u>Dominant</u> <u>Force</u>... The many are <u>ONE</u>!"

"Point taken." You've got to admit, when the Man makes his point, He *makes* a point, you know what I mean? I think my shoes are damp.

After a decent period of time to recompose myself, I queried on.

"Accepting, then, that some ultimate power actually *does* exist, the next logical issue which comes to mind would be: **Just wherein does the true strength of any deity lie?"**

As I think back on my own studies, over the years, I guess that, to any outside observer of life on the Earth, one would have to believe that man responds only to *fear*. Until the writings of Dr. Benjamin Spock, who examined the principles of child-rearing, many of the people of the Earth had held to that old adage of "Spare the rod, and spoil the child." How many times, in the process of discussing principles of control over human behavior, has one heard the phrase, "Put the fear of God in him?" This particular misquote of Biblical wisdom suggests that it is, indeed, God's will that Man be *punished* for any, and all, offenses, whether committed intentionally or not, and no matter the source of that behavior. One has also heard that "ignorance is bliss"; but, at the same time, one learns that "ignorance of the law is no excuse."

And so, if the belief that one is to follow a righteous path through life, in the hopes of eventually earning one's entrance into a better life in the "hereafter," is it also to be performed in response to a fear of some potentially horrendous punishment, such as Hades? It is very troubling that any force, which may profess to control Mankind so profoundly, and *for his own good*, would be based on such a harsh learning paradigm.

Understandably, yes...but *acceptable?*

After all, what would one guess to be the very first word that any child actually learns? If you guessed that it might be "mamma," or "pappa," I'm afraid that you'd probably be wrong. *Remember*, the infant's predominant process of learning is through mimicking those experiences which predominate in his environment.

Keeping this fact in mind, then, what would be the word which the infant would most likely hear the most, no matter what language is being spoken? The answer...**NO**!... "No, no, don't touch"... "No, no, don't do this"... "No, no, don't do that."

And so, once the child's vocal chords have matured and strengthened to the point that he or she may be capable of exercising them, the first word spoken would probably be the one which has been heard the most...No! But, it would be stated with affirmation, and with pride, at having been able to demonstrate to the loved ones that he has, indeed, been paying attention. This word, which *must* be of such great power that the loved one's emphasize it so strongly, and with such zeal, *must* certainly demonstrate one's tenderness and willingness to share.

"No!...You see; I've been paying attention...I return to you, my loving parents, all that you have so lovingly shared with me, in trying to protect me, and in your show of affection."

And what does the parent do in response? The parent is absolutely *horrified* at the infant's obvious rebelliousness, his defiance. To be so negative, and so disrespectful...terms which this little human would not be capable of understanding for years yet. All of a sudden, the adult's facial expression and physical gestures become tense, and rigid, which only send the infant the message which is diametrically opposite to that which he had been expecting.

"What the heck did I do wrong now?!!"

Once more it was Jehovah that addressed myself, and the group.

"My power, and my source, lie in the spirit of Man!
"I exist in the heart of Man, I am knowledge, I am belief, I am the faith which one blindly holds.

I am NOT an "external" force, which acts on the individual in the disciplinary manner which has been thus described.

My source, and my strength, lie within the individual...but my strength may be intensified, and focused, through the family."

He then focused back to me. "Many of the earliest forms of prayer were offered through the household deity, who protected the home, and the family within it. In its later forms, these household/family deities may have risen to the status of a *totem*, an anthropomorphized symbol, representing some particular group membership. Some of the characterizations were made in the form of the family ancestors, who were believed to continue life as part of this spirit, protecting and teaching the family in the ways of survival in this world. The family, or the clan, would raise their voices together, believing that this would intensify the message, and assure that the word would be heard.

"The later forms of the expression of religious belief focused on *silent* prayer, which would be offered by the individual, in solitude. This form of prayer might more closely relate to one's expression of personal *needs*, in the context of one's stresses in the real world, while not having to wait for a congregation to gather. However, there has usually been some kind of provision for group prayer, which also serves as a means for gathering people together, as well as offering the greeting to God. Perhaps, Man can unify, at least in terms of that for which he prays, even if he can rarely agree with others on anything else in life. Prayer, then, becomes an expression of a faith which is *shared* within the people of a group. I think that this may have been one of my better schemes, you know? Mankind fights over *everything*...so I thought I had to find something...*anything*...that might draw people together."

"What about that stuff, you know, about me being my brother's keeper? Did *you* have anything to do with that? Is that the only way I have of earning my wings, concentrating my life on the welfare of others?"

I'd always kinda wondered about that one, in particular. But I feared that, if I were to ask it, I might be opening myself to potential disaster. It would be like walking down the street, obsessively trying to avoid stepping on any cracks in the sidewalk. That's the surest way I've found of walking smack into a telephone pole, or something.

"Ever flown on an airline?"

What kind of question was this, now?

"Well, yeh. Sure."

"You remember the part where the flight attendant gives that spiel about the seatbelts, and what to do should the oxygen masks drop down in front of you?"

"Yeh! But, to tell you the truth, I'd probably shit my pants."

"No...Really? You know how they tell you that, if you're caring for someone with you, that you should affix your own mask *first*, and *then* help your partner? Think about it. If you don't take care of yourself first, the other person is most likely already panicking, and probably fighting you. You run out of air in the struggle, and you're *both* past tense.

"Well, I guess that *that's* what I was trying to convey.

"There's a passage which is often quoted in churches, which states that "He also helps them, that help themselves." If you righteously care for yourself, in this life, and maintain a healthy interaction with the world around you, then this may also be interpreted as your preparation of the world for others. If one relies on others, in any way, then one finds that what is good for the one, would be as good for the others. **Feed the heart, and the body will thrive**. So, what may start as faith and belief in one's Creator, which centers on the individual, will naturally flow to becoming the general good for all."

Each question seems to bring another more clearly into view. I was hoping I wasn't being seen as a "pest"; but I had been holding all these things in for so long.

"There's been a great deal of discussion, at least in the Christian and Islamic faiths, of this thing they call "*salvation*." I don't know that I've ever fully been able to grasp that, as a concept. What *is* salvation? Is there any special, or specific, means proscribed for attaining it? Is there some magic formula? Is there some singular accepted path toward the seeking of Eternity?

"I've heard each of the different groups defining this term in accordance with their own beliefs, and each seems to *exclude* the other. Some of them seem to be preaching a form of violence as a way of gaining entrance into Heaven. That sounds dubious to me. It sounds like they're saying "Love thy fellow man, but only if he believes exactly as you.""

Jehovah smiled, shook his head, and responded, "It's been presented, previously in our discussion, that behavior, alone, cannot be the only means by which an individual may seek his path through life. First of all, there have been many conceptions as to where the ultimate path may lead. For some, there is a *place*, in which one may exist *forever*. It carries many labels: Heaven, Valhalla, the Elysian Fields...In this place, one may experience only the positive, in comparison to the perils and strife which are brought to bear upon our earthly bodies.

"For others, who seek to raise themselves to the level of those whom they have revered, such as the followers of Buddha, there is the goal of being seated beside one's God, and being a part of that Heaven. In such a case, it is no longer the *destination*, but the *internal path*, which is of importance.

"In either case. One may note that one's actions, and one's behaviors, are so much a reaction to, and the result of, *circumstances* that it would be ill-suited as the sole path to what you have called Salvation. Mankind, being only the singular member of an entire animal kingdom, possesses inborn potentials and predications toward certain ways of responding to the world; and these proclivities may occur in the absence of choice. *Faith*, that quality of unquestioning belief, is something which is more self-directed, and comes from the inner core of each individual. Each individual is born with a relatively equal share of this quality; but, through life, one possesses the potential for cultivating it further.

"This *inner faith* tends to represent an element of *intent*, and is more than a simple measure of motivation. It may not be visible to the average observer. Even one's observable behavior, which may be the result of this intent, may offer little clue to that intent. That *intent* may wholly meet only their deity's established conditions, while the resulting behavior may actually fail miserably in the eyes of other mortals. It is faith which more fairly determines such factors, as Salvation."

"I'm sorry, again; but each step forward only urges me to seek even further. If one were to work ever so hard, and to live the holiest of lives possible, here on Earth, then *what* will be one's reward? Does one gain rewards in one's life on Earth, or are all rewards granted only once one has arrived in the *hereafter*?"

"You can have everything you want, as long as you don't want everything!"

Somehow, that's just the kind of answer I was expecting to get. He's consistent, you had to admit that. I guess that it's still up to myself to find some meaning in all of this. I remember Moses saying that the reward of a just life, was a just life. One performed for the good of Mankind, because that would be for the good of the individual, as well.

"OK, then; here's a good one for You. I'm sure You've become aware of all of the hoopla which is going on down there, in the Middle East...I mean Iraq, Iran, Afghanistan...I fear that Islam is one of those "mysterious" faiths, which generally fall within the purview of the ignorance of the non-Islamic peoples. Most of what the non-Islamic people have learned of Islam has been as a result of all the hostilities, starting, probably, with the Crusades, another great star in Man's history.

"Christians and Jews have habitually reacted to each other out of *fear*, because that is what they were *taught*. Islam has been perceived as a violent religion, which preaches the Holy Jihad, the war against *all* infidels; that is, all who do not believe as do the Moslems. Television newscasts focus their audiences on all of the negative qualities of anything which it covers. They keep repeating that any follower, who sacrifices his life for the honor of Allah, by destroying the power of the non-believer, will be granted so many virgins in the next life. Moreover, the honor will be shared with the family forever.

"Tell me...What kind of religion is *this*?

"Is *this* what God stands for?"

At this point, Mohammed himself stood, and stepped forward, a look of consternation on his face. Then, his face lightened a bit, and he said, "I remember once entering an establishment, and on the wall of this place was a placard. This placard read,

"I know that you understand what you think I said; but I'm not sure you realize that what you heard, is not what I meant."

"*I*, myself, don't have any memory of ever saying, or writing, *anything* which could be construed as supporting the commission of such violent acts as a means of gaining one's salvation."

Having made this statement, he turned his head, and looks all about him at the gathering. Then he asked, "Has anyone here *ever* dictated that such violence become a part of their belief system, and that it be carried out in His name?"

He turned back to me. "I would guess that the agent responsible for this element is, again, that magical, added ingredient, called *civilization*! Just think about that for a moment. The word "civil," itself, stands for something which is civilized, something which is polite, especially in matters which are neither religious nor military.

"I'm sorry, but I *refuse* to take credit, or blame, for some of the things that people may attribute to me out of their own ignorance. Besides, the television recites the declarations of the clerics, which state that those who die in the name of the Holy Jihad will have so many virgins in the next life. Oh, really! Where are they ever going to find *that* many virgins...even in the next world?"

And now, even more to digest. And it was getting close to dinner time, which would be tough enough to digest on its own. I could deal with only the one thing at a time; and my choice would be, dinner. After that, maybe I'd sit back, and reexamine all of this.

Chapter Twelve

It had been several days since I happened upon this setting, at least, that's the best estimate that I could make of the passage of time; and many of the questions I had always held about religion had been confronted. Whatever the practice of the rest of the world, it had always been my own style to first deal with the "generic," or the basic units of belief, those non-sectarian issues, which face one on the day-to-day journey through life.

When it came to any discussion of religious belief, one generally finds that the individual in our society tends to become fixated within the only school of thought to which he has been educated. We each have a tendency to *project* that which *we* believe onto others. As individuals, we are each considered as expressing a form of *narcissism*; as a *culture*, this would probably be labeled as *ethnocentrism*.

While I was a doctoral student in psychology, I chanced upon a professor, who had been raised in Europe, as the son of a very well educated and liberal family, in the area of Czechoslovakia. He reported that his parents had spent the early years of his life educating him in the basic principles of the world's major philosophies and theologies, believing that, in order for

one to make the most educated and most honest *choice* of belief systems to follow, a certain cognitive and intellectual ability would be required. My professor stated that he was able to
speak any number of languages, that he had been able to read
many of the original writings of each such heritage, in its native language, and was able to relate to these various approaches.
That which he *chose* for himself to follow turned out to be a
rather *generic* faith, a mixture of the ethereal and the worldly.

All of this had made sense to me at the time, while most of
the dogmatically singular belief systems, frankly, left me cold.
As a matter of fact, with the development of the "superstores"
in the business sector, with the end of the "blue laws," which
restricted trade on the Sabbath, and with the amalgamation of
many small businesses into the few giants, I had jokingly expressed my belief to friends that I had considered accepting
the leadership of one of these giants, and establishing *my own*
church, which I would name: **The First Church of the Generic God, and Discount House of Worship**. There would
be a giant yellow smiley-face over the entrance, and donations
could be made by credit card, at the door. There would be a
"greeter" at the door, who would direct each worshipper toward that section of the sanctuary which was most relevant to
his own desired interest, at least, on that particular day.

As I considered the concept of the "religious institution," I
found an old issue resurfacing in my consciousness. I had
never clearly understood the concept of "canonization" in the
organized Church; the process whereby a mere *mortal* could
actually become a *saint*, an individual whose attainment of
Heaven had been recognized by other mortals. More than just
this, Mankind had commonly taught his young to demonstrate
reverence for those individuals who had been recognized for
their leadership of that particular congregation. Many of these

so-called "leaders" have been heard to claim that they believed that they had been *chosen*, or had been *called*, to represent their fellow Man to God, or visa versa.

With all of this formulating in my head, I turned to the gathering and posed my question to the group, as a whole; "What, exactly, would be the proper way of addressing the recognized head of any congregation? I have found that many of these leaders tend to define their own role as being the leader of a "flock," which suggests that they would perceive the general following as little more than sheep, who, of necessity, would have to be "led" in one direction, or another.

"Others have stated that their "calling" had come *directly* from God, Himself. This, excuse me, sounds a little bit presumptuous, since the mere peasants of this Earth have no real means for verifying this point.

"My question, I guess, would have to involve the manner in which these self-defined "chosen" were, in fact *chosen* to represent God's word, here in Earth?"

There was suddenly a great deal of generalized commotion within the gathering; but it was, again, Jehovah who stepped forward.

"I can easily see the confusion under which you seem to be functioning. There appear to be so many such leaders, each defining their own position as being one which had been made directly by one of *Us*, the deities, and that they were summoned to such leadership through some form of "Divine Word." In reality, I can't remember ever having actually done that.

"Again, the confusion may relate to the conditions, and the functions, of the humanity under which such religious beliefs must be transmitted. As has been stated earlier, many cultures have, unfortunately, contaminated the arena of religion by infusing it with the politics of Man. Many have gone so far as to

define those in the political arena as, themselves, being deified. The emperors of Rome placed wreaths of laurel upon
their own heads, declaring themselves to be gods. Even as
recently as the British monarchies, of the Eighteenth Century,
any citizen could be severely disciplined for not averting his
eyes, and bowing his head, in the presence of the monarch."

From among those of Oriental ancestry, it was Lao Tse
who next approached the group.

"Greetings, honored guest. Let me introduce myself; I am
Lao Tse. Among the ancient civilizations, such as those of
China, India, Japan, there was offered a great reverence for
one's ancestors, which was demonstrated through both prayers
and offerings. Many of the religious rites which were practiced, were focused on this type of belief.

"However, this may have been performed more as a *questioning* offered up to one's ancestors, than as an actual *prayer*.
All humans have been confused about the path, which they are
to take through this life; and it was considered as a reasonable
practice to question those with the greatest experience in this
process of "living." One's ancestors, who had already proven
themselves to be successful in the endeavor, could be asked for
some form of guidance in the process of one's day-to-day living. This was offered as a sign of *respect*, but *not* on the same
level as one would offer in prayer to the very Maker of Life.
What say you, Buddha?"

"This is true, my friend. There are many sects which teach
their young to show this reverence for their elders, much less
one's ancestors. The elders, after all, possess the greatest experience in the art of survival. They have survived the hard-
ships, and have gathered the knowledge with which to challenge any future problems; and they have learned the most
valued means toward the task of one's daily survival. They

have, in fact, *earned* that reverence, which is paid to them, in their guarantees of survival, which have been passed down to their progeny. They are the teachers, who possess the knowledge on which the next generation may thrive."

"Teacher, you say! That is, indeed, the most powerful of positions to be held by any man. As a matter of fact, that is the very meaning of the word "Rabbi." It is the position of the greatest respect among the Jewish people. It is also through the leaders that the traditions, and the rights of passage, are handed down. They are the engineers of tradition and knowledge."

Having said this, Moses bows his head, and slowly strokes his beard. "It worries me to look upon the Earth today. I have noted that, in many cases, the role of the teacher has been usurped by the use of mechanical devices. Perhaps, within a few generations, the Rabbi may find that, when he opens the curtains of the altar, within the synagogue, there, before him, shall be a monitor; and, on the screen, only three letters will appear...IBM, instead of G-O-D!"

His expression was now saddened, as he held his head in his hands. "For those who have been recognized as the leaders of their congregations, there will be a diversity of function which they must serve. While some may be noted primarily for passing on the traditions of their beliefs alone, many shall demonstrate even greater responsibility, that of conveying the rules for healthy living, in general."

"And so, are these individuals recognized by *You* as *Your* representatives on Earth?" I asked of Jehovah.

In response, I heard a unified response from all congregated here; **"All of Man represents God!"**

"But, are they truly preaching the *Word of God*; I mean, as *You* intended it?"

"As we have already heard, there are those who have either accepted, or taken on, the task of leading mankind. Some have been of mortal birth, and some have been accepted as evolving from some unearthly source. However, in each one's role on Earth, the leaders of *Man* have been chosen from among those who are *mortal*, and have been selected *by mortals*. While, in their hearts, each may be sincere in his belief that he preaches the Word of God, each may not have been chosen directly by God.

"That which each of these representatives may hold in common is the *intent* of their chosen position. Each may sincerely believe that he conveys the Word of God, as God had intended it to be passed on. One can only hope that the most sincere of these individuals are able to carry out the defined wishes of his deity."

To be perfectly honest, I, as an individual, had always maintained some suspicion about the motives of some of these leaders. Granted, there are many whom I believed to be in earnest. However, there have also been many whose very *humanness* just *oozed* out of every pore. While many had called upon Mankind to cast his bread upon the water, there have also been those who have, I've noted, buttered their own bread.

"How, then, are we, as mere mortals, to know those who would teach us *Your* meanings?"

"I don't believe that there exists any one singular true test," said Jehovah. "One must remember that there are many who may believe that their deluded thoughts are actually those of the deity that they profess to serve and represent. Some religious groups demand that those who represent their deity be free of the encumbrances of humanity, such as material wealth, or the conflicting desires of the human body. The fact that these individuals would be willing to make such sacrifices may convince many common folk of the sincerity and holiness of these individuals. However, as one might readily take note, from recent TV and newspaper reports, many who have taken on the frock of God are only *too* human."

"So, what, then, can we trust? It is one thing to conceive of a deity, or to choose a manner in which one is to lead one's life, which appears to be personal issues; or, perhaps, an issue between the individual and his chosen deity. But, it is another thing to select that individual who will represent one's faith, possibly as an intermediary between oneself and that deity," I thought.

"Maybe, **that's** the point of all of this! Maybe the person that is chosen to unite the congregation, and to transmit "The Word," is simply *that*, a *person*, and is not to be given any more power or significance than *that!*"

Jehovah leans forward, and, with a hand on my shoulder, he says, "I hear your thoughts, my son...and I concur. The granting of humanity to Man was, indeed, a great gift, I believe; and, by sacrificing these gifts in order to accept a leadership role, one is, in reality, offering a gesture of his surrender of his *humanity*, that very same privilege which has been offered to every human on Earth.

"Of course, it is also possible that one could perceive this as a *snubbing* of that gift, which has been given by the deity. Besides, there is no real way in which anyone can give up his humanity. One *always* remains human, and shall possess all of the same needs and instincts which are common to all of humanity.

"One finds that, in many cultures, those who lead the congregation have been chosen from among the prominent families of the community. For some, it could be considered as an honor that the eldest child would dedicate one's life to the

Church, and, in so doing, bring honor to the family's name. For others, the life of the clergy could be a form of escape from whatever horrors one was seeking to hide from. In many of these cases, it may have been an involuntary gesture by which the position was taken; and, in these cases, it may have been demanded of the individual that he must *deny* his personal desires. Many, who may have had a troubled past, only carried those psychological scars with them into the clergy, never to be honestly cleansed.

"Among the followers of Buddha, however, the priesthood is open to each and every individual. It is the right, and the expectation, of each individual, to take his/her turn within the priesthood, which is perceived as a cleansing of one's Earthly weaknesses. This process is freely supported by the entire population, each taking his turn, before returning to the mundane tasks of life and family. None are "chosen"; but all serve their duty to God, as well as to one's fellow man."

"Are you saying, then, that those who choose that role, as leader of that particular faith, or who are, in some way, supposedly "chosen" for that role, are not really representing God?"

Once more, Jehovah took a moment to compose his thoughts, before turning again toward the questioner. "In truth, as *I* see it, *each person* both represents, and *celebrates*, God in his own way.

"Those who take on the recognized role as a leader of the faith, or the leader of a congregation, may be variously identified as a "priest," and called a "man-of-the-cloth," or a "man-of-God." Among the Protestant faiths, the minister is a member of the congregation, who has been authorized by that congregation to conduct the religious services, and to manage the physical plant. In its original form, the Jewish faith had no formal "leader," per se; each man in the congregation would take his turn leading the daily prayers. As a matter of fact, this process continues in the more Orthodox settings. The term, "Rabbi," stands for "teacher," and is the individual who has been trained to educate the members of the congregation.

"Of course, with the evolution of "institutions" within society, the organizations of Man, and his activities, have become ever so much more complex. Just as nations, and governments, may require special handling, so have the various religious groups. And so, those that represent the religious groups may also be taking on certain social and organizational functions. For example, I have become aware that the Roman Catholic Church has become one of the largest financial institutions in the world, with holdings in cash and real properties. One does not allow any haphazard management of such funds."

"Wow! Money really *is* power, isn't it! If that really is so, then wouldn't it seem to be terribly unfair for the Church to seek so many economic sanctions from the governments? If what You say is true...and, believe me, Lord, the last thing I want to do is to challenge You!...then the Church may be at least as wealthy as many countries themselves! Is it fair that they should be given this kind of special privilege?"

"Well, you know, in their origins, most of the recognized religions were more than simply a symbol of faith to their followers. The churches were a source of nurturance, both figuratively, and realistically. In the Great Depression of the American 1930's, it was the Church activity which helped to support the people. Even later, there evolved the phenomenon of the "soup kitchen," and "shelters," and other charitable functions which were practiced by the Church, for those who could not survive on their own.

"In today's society, many of these churches have organized and, unfortunately, institutionalized into such organizations as the Catholic Charities, which appear to operate very much as the governmental units, which serve the same functions. Where it had once been the individual who gave freely of himself for the good of humanity, and in the name of charity, it is now a licensed agency, with all its regulations and criteria, which serve the needs of Man.

"The Church now seems to be taking on the trappings of the cultures which they serve, from functioning as teachers, to involvement in the day-to-day functioning of the individual. The Church has been dealing in such things as properties, tithes, dues, fees, and such "taxing" of its members, much as any government would do. In light of all this, I must agree with your view on their tax-deferred, or tax-exempt, status.

"Perhaps, one would be best to limit one's perception to the saving of souls, or to the charities which serve Mankind, as the best parts to be protected from government control, especially in such countries as the United States, where the Constitution guarantees the separation of Church and State. But, even this can become a fuzzy issue, especially in those cases in which a national leader takes his role as one of being in the pulpit, and suggesting that, perhaps, _he_ believes that _I_, God, that is, may be talking directly to him. Those areas of the institution of the Church which are in the business of doing business, may be overstepping their bounds by demanding the protection which is best allowed to its religious functions."

"Here, here; I'm with You on that," I yelled in support. "It's no secret that many of the greatest religious structures in the world are on what might be considered to be _prime_ real-estate. And, many of the churches own vast holdings, which may have either been purchased by them, or granted, and handed down to them through gifting and inheritances. I've always had a hard time accepting the fact that rental properties could be free of taxation of some sort.

"And, while we're dealing with *questionable* issues, such as that of special privilege, maybe this could be the time to raise the question of the "Afterlife." There have been so many presentations on the role which each of us plays on this Earth, and the location to which we may each be heading...eventually, that is. It was noted earlier that one of the reasons for the Reformation of the Church had to do with the purchasing of favor by the wealthy, a way of buying entrance into Heaven, as it were, or whatever it is that one seeks. Are we looking at Heaven, or Hell?"

"You're talking in terms of Christianity, again," answered Jehovah. "There are so many paths which one can follow; and we have tried, each in our own way, to guide Man toward a purification of the soul.

"Let me offer some of the other deities an opportunity to answer this question...Moses? Why don't you take a shot at it?"

"I can only speak for the Old Testament, remember, and the Judaic culture, which followed it. The Old Testament certainly talks about the Devil. The Old Testament tells the story of how he was at odds with God, and, for his defiance of The Law, he was cast out of Heaven. It then became *his* role to tempt Man into joining him in defying The Law. However, Judaism tends to focus more on the "righteous path" for Mankind to take than it does on the casting of one's soul into Hell.

"In the Old Testament, the instructions which were given to Man have directed him to seek after God's presence, to understand His meaning and purpose, in *this* world...and for living the life which God had prescribed for Man. The rewards for leading "the right life," generally, were just that...it was that he would be able to lead the "right life." True, man could be rewarded with Eternity; but the real focus was on the "here-and-now."

"J.C.? What would you add to this topic?"

"The Christian Doctrine, as you know, is based on the New Testament, the reported writings of *my* teachings, as presented by my disciples. The New Testament is more actively involved with an apparent "rewards system," which would include both positive and negative reinforcements. On the negative side, one is threatened with eternal damnation for failure to follow that proscribed path, which leads to God. One might say that life on Earth could be defined as "sacrifice," in an effort at gaining that which *would* be forthcoming *if* one, indeed, led the right path through life.

"In the beginning, there was only the presence of God; that's all that one learns from the readings. However, one must also understand that the *angels* existed with him, in the purity of their ethereal souls. Thus, there had to be souls, which existed *before* the Creation, and the Garden of Eden, in which were created Adam and Eve.

"The Devil, you see, was one of those souls. He couldn't, or wouldn't, follow the rules which had been established for *all* to follow; and, for this, he was cast out of Heaven. His response to the fall from *Grace* was to create a realm of his own. And thus, it had to be God who had created *both* Heaven and Hell. Thereafter, Man was presented *choices*, which could be influenced by the Devil, as well as by God. The Devil's temptations of Man, you see, were designed as his way of getting even for his punishment.

"But, there are other beliefs which relate to the "afterlife," are there not?"

I then recognize a deity who could only be Krishna; but I am embarrassed to say that this recognition was more from my experiences at airports than from reading the literature. I'm glad to say that *this* Krishna presented himself in a much more dignified manner.

"It is, I believe, the emphasis of most religious systems of thought to teach each man to focus his life, here on Earth. One is instructed in the ways of living one's life to a particular standard, which can be seen as most productive and rewarding, for oneself, as for one's family.

"One might say that the individual's functions in this life would best befit the motto of some of the television advertisements for the United States Army, which states that the goal for each candidate is to be "All that one can be." In this way, each individual may be compared to that standard which he, alone, has established.

"It is the goal for the followers of Buddha to become "one" with the Buddha; which is not to say that they actually seek to become a "deity" themselves. Rather, it is through the purification of the soul, which is a process that takes place throughout the many cycles of the "Wheel-Of-Life," that one is finally given the opportunity of settling to rest in the Elysian Fields, or any of the other names which exist for that heavenly place. However, even here, upon one's seemingly having attained that certain perfection of the soul, one continues to have the opportunity of exercising *choice*, and once more returning to their mortal core, and to assist, or educate, the rest of Mankind.

"Isn't it an act of "pure love" to be able to give of oneself in this way? Material things, and physical acts, are only fleeting things, which one is capable of "measuring," and which can typically be replenished; but, with the demands which the individual may hear placed upon him from so many sources in this world, one can easily become confused over exactly what it is that a person is *supposed* to do.

"The **Self** maintains the wealth of one's soul, and remains above all attempt to measure it."

"But" I asked, "it is one thing for a deity to attain some pinnacle of functioning; but, wouldn't it be presumptuous for some mere mortal to seek this same stature? That's all very comforting, I'm sure; but, if one does not feel that one might be facing some imaginable consequence, as the result of one's chosen actions, right here on Earth, then how might a person be convinced to act in a certain way? Certainly, it would be *nice* to be *nice*; but, from my own limited body of experience, I have noted that most people are motivated by what's in it for them."

Krishna was quick to reply. "While many of these philosophies do not necessarily embody an actual place in which the body, or the soul, will find only "torment," much like the Hell of which you have spoken, they may instead consider that the return to this mantle of mortality is the greatest thing one might dread.

"There have even existed legends of some far better place in which the soul could potentially find peace; and so, the return to the Earth, to live out another cycle of life may, in itself, be perceived as something of a hell as well. One is said to "suffer humanity" in one's effort at rising above it.

"That philosophy that you have posed, reminds one of the Hindu way of life. In *that* philosophical system, there are "castes," into which each individual may fit. In theory, there exist three separate levels of human existence. The Brahman, or the priest class, exist at the upper level of the social order, and are thus much closer to Nirvana. At the lowest end, are the

"Untouchables," who have the longest journey, and are at the lowest rung of the ladder."

"Each individual is compared only against his *own* capacities; and, if able to attain *one's own* optimal level of functioning, within *this* life cycle, one may be returned to the mortal state, but, this time around, starting at a higher caste. As you can see, this is something of a "merit reward system." However, if one should falter at any point in the cycle, he may be returned at a lower caste in his next life. The final prize is the privilege of rising outside of this process of cycling, and having the opportunity of entering Nirvana. Whatever it is that the individual may attain in this life, one must not look at this life as being a "one-shot opportunity," as is conceived in the Western philosophies, which seems to present life as a one-time, winner-take-all situation. The individual is presented with an endless number of opportunities for attaining this state of Grace, if you will."

Thus dealt with, I exclaimed, "Well, so much for where one may eventually reside, God willing."

"Thank you" responded Jehovah.

"You're welcome, I'm sure," I replied. "But I still have a few questions about *where* this whole thing got its start. The Old Testament describes the story of Adam and Eve, representing the first "humanoids" on this planet, Earth. Furthermore, "Creationism" suggests, then, that the entire world had to be populated with *their* progeny...Am I right?"

"So?" asked Moses.

"So?...Don't you see, it relates to everything we've been admonished for by the Bible itself! If there were really only these *two* people, then that would necessarily make all of

Mankind...how to state this most delicately?...shall we say, *directly related*?"

"So?" asked Jesus.

"From all that I've been able to cajole from all of the religious literature that I've read, and from most of the major religious groups, that would most certainly be a big no-no. Just the thought of it brought to mind, "Oh, Brother!"...but, then again, *that's* just the point! I'm sure you've all heard this same argument many times, and from all kinds of people; but *I've* never received a plausible answer."

The others stepped aside on this one, and let Jehovah face the issue.

He stepped forward, picked up something from the ground, and held it as if it were a microphone. He held it to his mouth.

"That reminds me of a story...This guy walks into a bar...," and everyone put their hands to their mouths, and let out a big "Booooooo," in unison.

"No...wait, wait...This guy walks into a bar, and he tells everyone that he's been studying population statistics for a newspaper article that he's been writing. He states that he was listening to a radio program, and on it, there was a report that, somewhere on the Earth, every *three seconds*, a woman was giving birth."

Everyone was now of rapt attention, as Jehovah went into a long hesitation. "So, what the heck did he learn?"

"As the writer finished this statement, one of the men at the other end of the bar, and obviously over-lubricated, spewed forth the contents of his mouth, slammed his glass down on the bar, and shouted "For Christ's sake, we gotta find that woman, and *stop* her!"

Once again, there was a unified "Booooo" from the audience.

But Jehovah was undaunted. "No...seriously; this is actually a fair question regarding Creation. I guess it is a little rough when you read it just the way it's presented in the Bible. It's sometimes important to be able to read something *into* that section of the Bible, so that it may present itself as somewhat more complete. As it's presented, it may be a little terse. If it is indeed true, that all of life as we know it, began with just the two of them, then, maybe, we just *gotta* make childbirth an Olympic event.

"I'm afraid that this particular subject has presented a great deal of conflict from the very beginning. That which may be missing from that text is the *presumption* that there *had to be* life *outside* of the Garden of Eden. We've mentioned that there were already souls in My company, the Devil having been one who was unable to live by the rules of that establishment, and was cast out. I guess that what we're saying here, is that, while other people most definitely would have had to be living on the face of the Earth, Adam and Eve were the two who had been *selected* to be given special advantage over the rest. They were offered so much that others did not have; but only on the one condition, that they could *resist* some of the other temptations which the Garden of Eden held."

"So? What happened?" I asked.

"Well, it brings to mind a familiar saying, which states that "The mind was willing, but the flesh was weak." Where the Hell...pardon Me...do you think *that* came from?"

"I guess. But, what about that claim, of creating the Heavens and the Earth in just six days? You couldn't have been using *union labor*! I'll just bet that You just *had* to rest on that seventh day!"

Jehovah smiled. "So, whose calendar are you using?"

"Whadda Ya mean?"

"There are all kinds of calendars. Many of them existed long before there were any kinds of standards for measuring the days, or years. I think it was the Egyptians that really started to grasp the significance of "heavenly bodies"...other than Cleopatra's, that is...ha-ha-ha! No, really; the Egyptians were really pretty good astronomers. Then there was the Hebrew calendar; that dates back about 6000 years. The one which is most prominently used today, is the one established by Pope Gregory, which is why it's called the Gregorian Calendar; and it dates back just 2005 years, in *human time* that is."

"What do You mean, "human time"? Time is just time."

"Not so.

"*My* calendar is, of necessity, something completely different. Do you have any idea of what existence might be if there were no other souls with which to share anything with? Can you just *imagine* such an isolated existence?

"*That's* why I created that which I created, whether it be *here* on the Earth, or somewhere, throughout the multitude of universes out there. Lacking any true point of reference, there would have never been a need for such concepts as *time*. Why, it was just a few seconds ago...for *me*,...that your entire solar system even appeared.

"So, you see; *those* six days were *my* six days!...And, speaking of time, it would appear that ours has just run out. I can see Mog, down there, doing his little dance around the end of the fire; so, I'm guessing it must be getting pretty close to dinner time, again."

He was right, as I could hear the gurgling of stomachs around me. But I also noticed that the supply of food was starting to become more scarce, which was a sign that this group might have overstayed its welcome in this particular spot. Perhaps it would be time to move on.

As for myself, I hadn't really been planning on going anywhere. After all, I really wasn't sure just where "here" was, anyway. Up to this point, I hadn't experienced any necessity for plotting my journey. I was just feeling comfortable in being a part of this collection of souls...Oh! Did *I* say that!!!

No one had yet made any mention of a particular destination; only that they had been on some sort of "journey." The place at which we had congregated had only been intended as a minor rest-stop along the way. They had been kind enough to welcome me to join them, and to be a part of their life for the few days I was here.

But, I guess, now it would have to be up to *me* to make some kind of plan.

Where should I go from here...wherever *here* is...here...z-z-z-z-z?

Chapter Thirteen

It was a misty morning when I finally rose from my slumber, wiping the grains of dream-dust from the corners of my eyes. I was as yet in a fog, when I detected the scurry of busy hands and feet all around me. First, I took the moment to stretch, in an attempt at getting some of my blood out to my extremities; I scratched my belly, yawned, and then wiped my eyes again. When I finally took the time to look about me, I noticed that my companions seemed to be busily breaking camp, and getting ready to continue their journey.

"Wait!" I shouted.

"What?" was the united reply.

"Wait; we're not *finished*, yet."

"Finished?...Finished with *what*, exactly?"

They were right! In truth, we had never really *started* anything; at least, not *formally*. All I could remember was waking up, and finding myself...*somewhere*...I don't know where! None of *this* had been by design...at least, not by *my* design. I just sort of fell into this situation.

"Uhhh...Well, we're not finished with our discussion on the beliefs of Mankind...You know, where he's headed...where he came from...why he *is* what he *is*...!"

"Who promised that *you* would be the one to get all the answers?

We don't even have all the answers."

"But, there's still so much that I don't understand."

"Ah, so; do you know what *that* proves?" asks Jesus.

"No...What? Clue me in."

"It only proves that you're *human*. Think about it; what human has ever had all of the answers? Oh, sure, there have been those who *claimed* to know it all. But, *I*, myself, don't know it all," said Buddha. "No one can know it all, at least, not until *it is all to be known!* *"Everything"* has not happened, yet! Who can ever know that which is not yet to be known?"

"But...but...there's so *much!*"

Jehovah offered a supportive smile, as he said, "I'll tell you what; go ahead, and take your best shot! We've got a few minutes before we've got to go our separate ways. Go ahead...ask me whatever comes to your mind."

"Uhhhhhhhh...Mmmmm.........Uhhhhhh..."

"Good start, kid," offered Moses. "Maybe you could try and clear that up a bit...maybe add a couple of *words*, so we can start to make some kind of sense out of it."

"OK...Of all the things that You've done...and, by this, I mean the *collective* You...and out of *all* that You've created...what would You say is Your greatest feat? Was it the creation of human life?"

"Yeh, *that* was good."

"Aw, come on. You said that You'd at least try to be serious here!"

"Well, to be honest, the Holy Books...and, by this, I mean *all* of those who have claimed to report *My* word...have given My answer. I try to show no favorites. I love *all* that I have created; it's a small weakness I have. You won't tell anyone, will you?"

"Come on; You're copping out on me, aren't You? You just don't *want* to answer the question."

"Hey, wait a minute here! I *used* to show favoritism. It was long ago, before any of *this* was even a consideration. There was just Me...and the Spirits...You know, what the humans call "angels?" There was this one; a real spitfire. He had personality, and humor...and, boy, could he cook."

"So, what happened?"

"Oh, come on; you know the story. Once he realized that he had gotten onto My better side, he began to take advantage of the situation. I *tried* to be fair, so I couldn't allow this to get out of hand. The others were really getting annoyed."

"And?"

"Like a father with his son, I sat him down, and I told him that there would have to be *limits* set."

"What happened next?"

"He didn't like "limits." So, he kept testing Me. Finally, when it became evident that he wasn't about to stop this behavior, I **had** to discipline him. It was for the greater good of everyone."

"So, I guess that *that* fixed it...right?"

"Unfortunately, no. I'll let you in on a little secret; I had already started to create Mankind by this time, and I had been using *him* as my model. But, he didn't want to have any limits set on him; and he continued to run out of control."

"What happened next?"

"I had to cast him out."

"**Oh!....Him!**"

"Yeah, him. It taught me something about Man, as well. I guess that it's a story heard from many a wife over the centuries...*A man is as faithful as his options!* Believe Me, I've had to work hard to keep that thought in mind when responding to all those prayers and demands I regularly receive."

"How did You try to control this...in Man, I mean?"

"It was a matter of a little genetic engineering. But that got out of hand, too. You know all that stuff about the X and the Y chromosome?"

"I mean, yeah, sure."

"Well, you see...I left it kinda *unbalanced.*"

" How do you mean?"

"I meant to put in a Y-negative chromosome, too."

"What do You mean, a y-negative?"

"Can't you see? Every time you have a **why**, somebody always comes up with a **why not**!"

"You're pulling my leg, aren't You?"

"Hey! Maybe we've just been able to come up with an answer to your last question."

"What question?"

"The one about the creation which *I* liked *the best* of all I had created."

"And?"

"**BURLESQUE!!!** I just can't get enough of it. I really felt sad when vaudeville went on the skids, man. I thought that guy, Ed Sullivan, was gonna keep it going, with his show, The Toast of the Town. Too bad. Hey! Maybe *that's* where we'll witness a "second coming"!

"Second coming?"

"Yeah! Of burlesque. What did you *think* I meant?"

This guy just *had to be* the Almighty; He just had all the moves. To think, that people have been so terrified at the thought of meeting their Maker, worried at how they might be judged. If only they knew what kind of guy He is!

I sat back, and reflected on the last few days...or, more correctly, I guess, *my* last few days...who knows what the time-frame might have been for...You-Know-Who?

There had been a great deal of diversity presented and described, many points of view; and I had never really witnessed any great conflict. Any time the issue of anger, or violence, had been raised, especially with regard to *them*, they all seemed to appear confused. None of them could remember *violence* as part of their formula for Mankind. *That* seemed to have been one of the elements added on by Mankind, itself.

While I had had the honor of experiencing many of the belief systems of Man, and their deities, in this congregation, it had always seemed that they spoke as if of one voice. They always presented themselves as being hopeful and positive, and each seemed to have wished to allow Mankind a great deal of freedom to express himself as he chose.

For sure, the deities had offered some serious guidelines, much as one might expect from a loving parent, who was sending a child out into the world, after having offered each one the skills which they would need to survive. However, it was always up to the child, itself, to make the best use of these skills. Once the child had grown to the point that he could leave the crib, the child would have to learn to feed himself. The parent, of course, would remain nearby, observing, in the background, just in case some help would be needed. But, even then, it would be up to each child to *ask* for that help...and to be able to recognize that help once it was offered.

Like most kids, Mankind had a habit of taking a lot for granted. He rarely said "Thank you" for anything he got, and might believe that he actually owed nothing to anyone.

There is also the fact that the deities never appeared to have planned on Mankind's art of *institutionalizing* everything. Mankind just couldn't pass up an opportunity to *organize* that which he had been given as a gift, and placing that inimitable *human* stamp on it. Mankind could never leave religion in the form of a philosophy; they had to *organize* it, to *compartmentalize* it, to *regulate* it, to *define* it...In the end, it was nearly unrecognizable.

I was suddenly roused from my reveries by the commotion once more, and realized the position in which I now found myself.

"So...What do I do now?"

"That's completely up to you," advised Krishna. "Nobody's made any demands on you to this point, have they? Ever hear of "self-determination?" Even if you believe in predestination, or that everything has already been preordained, that which will be...will be."

"And, so...What you're saying is...?"

"Go with the flow...Be at ease with the breeze...Take a walk on the wild side," was the response from Lao Tse. "Life, my friend, is a smorgasbord; enjoy it, and don't just settle for the first meatball that shows up on your plate."

I thanked Him...or is it Them?...for the advice, and I watched as they gathered their things together, and slowly started walking into the mist. All of the others had already made their way part way across the field, so Jehovah picked up His pace, in order to catch up. He turned to me, for just a second; and He said, "It's been real....," and then He turned, and went on his way.

At first, the field appeared to be filled with all of these characters. I could see the Sun reflect off the armor, which was being worn by Joan-of-Arc. The Norse gods were making a great deal of noise banging their shields with their battle-hammers. Moses kept looking behind him, as if he'd left something behind. He had two large tablets in his arms, and he was acting as if there might be something more that he was supposed to be carrying.

And, near the center of the pack, I could detect some commotion. When I looked, I could see my old friend, Mog, chasing something, again. What a guy!

But then, I blinked my eyes, for just a second; and, when I looked, there were only a few figures visible on the field.

I blinked, again; and there were fewer yet.

When I finally stopped, to wipe my eyes, in an effort at getting a better look at them, there was only the singular figure, standing there, alone, in the middle of the field.

I realized that I still was not completely satisfied with the answers which I had received. After I thought about it for another moment, I asked myself if, maybe, I had been asking the wrong questions. So, I cupped my hands to my mouth, and I yelled out, "Wait a minute. Tell me, with all of Your power, and all of Your intelligence, why is it that this world is still so screwed up?"

The lone figure suddenly stopped in His tracks, and stood there motionlessly for a second. Then, He turned, very slowly, with a sad smile on His face. He shrugged His shoulders, and

He said, **"WHADDA YA WANT? AFTER ALL, WE'RE ONLY HUMAN!"**

Then, He waved, turned slowly, and walked out of view.

While He was the only figure which had become visible to me, still, I could hear chuckling, as if it was coming from all around me.

Then, it was *my* turn; so I started back in the same direction from which I had come.

Chapter Fourteen

Alone!...I'm all alone!

In a world that's filled with Christians, and Roman Catholics, and Protestants, and Orthodox, and Anglicans, and Muslims, and Hindus, and Buddhists, and Sikhs, and Jews, and Ba'Jais, and Confucionists, and Jains, and Shintoists, and Taoists, and Zoroastrianists, and atheists...and I'm alone!

Well, if the last few days have taught me anything, it would probably be the fact that *no one* is ever truly *alone*...as long as that is not his avowed *choice*. The true test of one's beliefs is carried in the heart, not in the wallet, or in the temple, or in one's actions.

The real strength is in the "belief," whatever that belief may be. It does not demand that an individual identify some specific symbol, or recognize any official organization, which may be connected with that belief. Although many religions pray in a group, or a congregation, the silent prayer is just as powerful.

Even those individuals who have spent a lifetime in denial of any personal belief in God, at that moment at which they may find that they have totally lost control over this world, and are losing their cool, *then* do they seek out some form of deity, and beseech this deity for protection. As one approaches the natural end to one's life, no matter what one had preached to that day, one will seek some guide to the other side, or some comfort at facing this change in one's energy form. Even the non-believer seeks to "hedge his bets" by offering praise to the deities, a form of insurance of some form of pay-back for an investment made in life.

Even for those individuals placing a curse on others, there is often some cooperation sought from the deities in carrying out some devastation upon their person, or their progeny. In its simplest form, it is but the mildest recognition that here is, indeed, a power which does exist, in some form. Just listen, the next time someone near you sneezes. Inevitably, there will be the automatic blessing offered, by rote. The actual source of this act was evolved out of Medieval superstition, which suggested that the sneeze was, in fact, the body's attempt at expelling the Devil from within.

Along with the Russian Revolution, at the turn of the Twentieth Century, and with the development of the Communist Party, there was a great deal of talk about the "godless" Commies. Between Karl Marx and Frederick Engels, there was a lot of talk about religion being perceived as the "opiate of the masses," which only served to blind men from seeing the reality of their existence. But, even when some political force had sought to pull the rug out from under religion, as a force among the people, that same politic also sought to place *itself* in that very same role, and asked the people to pay reverence to its leadership.

The emperors of Rome deified themselves, and declared holidays to celebrate themselves. Any leader, who was seeking the support of the people, often allied himself with the churches which were most dominant in their countries.

But, do you know what? Even with all the information they could muster, at their disposal, and with the confirmation of any of the beliefs which I may have always held, I still have absolutely no idea where in the hell I am...and even less awareness of the direction in which I *should* be headed!

Yup...alone...that's what I am.

If I were Dorothy, in <u>The Wizard Of Oz</u>, all I'd have to do is to tap the heels of my ruby slippers together, three times, and incant "There's no place like home"; and I'd open my eyes, and be back in the loving arms of my family and friends. The only trouble with that is that I don't think they make orthopedic ruby slippers, with a four-inch lift on the left heel.

So, I guess I would have to just pick some direction to walk, and continue in that direction until I have arrived...but where?...and which direction?

Noticing that the fire still had some embers glowing, I decided to gather some brush with which to stoke the fire. I made myself a comfortable little spot, so I might just sit back, and try to think this thing out, before making any kind of decision, which I might regret later. So, I propped myself up near the fire, threw a few more twigs on the embers so that I could bring the flames back, and I leaned back into the seat I had made.

I was trying to mentally rework some of the things which I had been experiencing, and trying, somehow, to fit them into the philosophy of life that I'd managed to eke out for myself over the years. I wondered how I might be able to improve upon the direction which my life was taking. I did a lot of chewing, but was having some trouble when it came to actually "digesting" it all.

I leaned my head back a bit, resting it on some soft tree boughs, and was relishing the aroma of the pine that was emanating from them. I closed my eyes...just briefly...just to bring all my senses to bear on the comfort which I was feeling at that moment...

The next thing I knew, I could hear a noise, which I felt was familiar, and it sounded as if it were just above my head. When I looked up, I could see the old heating vent hanging from the ceiling, blowing down on me, and blowing my hair around.

I opened my eyes, and I could see the computer screen flickering, right there in front of me. I almost fell over backwards in the leather office chair, on which I found myself perched.

I was back in the office!

I took the moment to glance at my wrist, and I noticed my watch, just like it had been in the past. Moreover, and according to the latest in Timex technology, it appeared that there had only been **five minutes** elapsed since I had last looked at it.

But, that can't be ...That *had* to be *days* ago!

If I hadn't been disoriented before, I was now.

Who...what...where...when...?!!!

I swiveled around in the chair, and I took a long look around me. The office appeared to be exactly the same as I had remembered it. Nothing had changed...except for *me*, that is.

I stood up, and immediately had to reach for my cane, as my knee gave out on me. Nothing new there, either.

I looked down, and I could see a set of dirty footprints, which ran along the carpet, and went halfway across the room.

That's *weird*...The marks only *begin* halfway across the floor, and then lead toward my desk. I looked down at my feet, and I found that there was some kind of dirt on my shoes as well...along with some pine needles, just like those on which I had been sitting...or, at least, thought I had been sitting...or, was I?

But, I'm *sure* that it all happened, exactly as I remember it. I was *there*, wasn't I?!!

Hey! Wait a minute...**You** were there, too; weren't you?!!

Don't go looking around you; you know who I'm talking to...I'm talking to **you**!

No! You're not just going to close the book, and try to put this out of your mind.

You can't just leave me like this!

There are still too many questions which have been left unanswered.

If you were really paying attention, then you've *got* to help me answer some of these questions.

I'll tell you what...Why don't you jot down the name and the address of this publisher. And, after you've taken some time to more fully digest this book, I'd appreciate your taking a shot at answering the question I asked that "last man standing," so to speak...remember?...Out there in the mist?

What question, you ask?

You remember, don't you?

After I had tried to piece together all of the information and ideas which I had gained from that encounter with the deities, I then realized that they really had had no differences among them, at least on the important things.

My question was: With all that Mankind held in common,

HOW COME THE WORLD WAS STILL SO SCREWED UP?

I'll tell you what; if you take the time to respond to this question, in writing if you please, I'll accept your signature on the note as a "release," so that, should I write an answer to *this* book, and I use *your* ideas or words, I promise to give *you* the credit for those thoughts.

Is that fair, or what!

Hey, if that whole process worked for this particular question, then what if I just lean back in my chair...and start thinking...about...Playboy Magazine!!!

Z-z-z-z-z-z-z-z-z-z-z-z-z-z-z-z-z-z-z-z...

About the Author

Michael Raskin is the product of New Jersey, and a student of psychology, anthropology, and archaeology, who earned a doctorate in psychology. After more than 25 years working at a mental health center in Maine, he started his own private practice, in a small village, where he was able to muse on some of the basic questions facing Man. His first two novels followed a Northern Maine farm boy through his misadventures in the US military. Not being one for avoiding challenges, he chose to examine man's evolution in biological, social, economic, political, and religious arenas of life.

Printed in the United States
47233LVS00003B/121-195

9 781594 083945